Max–
Canine Concierge of Love

MARIAH LYNNE

MAX - CANINE CONCIERGE OF LOVE
Copyright © 2023 by Mariah Lynne

ISBN: 979-8-88653-127-5

Published by Satin Romance
An Imprint of Melange Books, LLC
White Bear Lake, MN 55110
www.satinromance.com

Published in the United States of America.

Cover Design by Caroline Andrus

To Max our wonderful dog who shared fifteen years of his unconditional love with us. He loved everyone he met, visited nursing homes, did a magic show for our island kids, and loved to bark at dolphins. His antics, adventures, and love of life inspired this story.

And to all the Service Dogs whose love, loyalty, and guidance help people with all types of disabilities every day, this story is in honor of them.

"All dogs are therapy dogs. Most are just working undercover."

— AUTHOR UNKNOWN

CHAPTER
ONE

I've never bit anyone. Never wanted or had to. I love everyone I meet. That's what humans love about me and my love for them is what brought me to my forever home.

"Max," Nate, my doggie dad, whispered as he stroked my fur. "Come on, buddy, wake up. Today's your big day. You're going to be the center of attention. We need to get you groomed. After all, you're the reason for today's celebration."

I stretched and yawned, waking up excited there was another wedding at The Two Turtles Inn. I already knew that because yesterday on my walk with a guest, a nice elderly lady named Mrs. Gray, we stopped to watch the maintenance staff assemble the wedding trellis and place the wooden folding chairs on The Inn's expansive front lawn facing the calm blue-green waters of the Gulf of Mexico.

Nate fed me a hearty breakfast before we walked to The Inn's spa to visit my groomer, Georgia. Excited to greet her, I headed straight for her waiting open arms. As she smiled, her face flushed with love as she looked into my eyes. "Max, I'm going to make you look even more gorgeous than ever." Georgia, a pretty woman in her thirties, had fine light-colored long hair tied back with a Turtle Inn ribbon.

She was short, which I loved because I could easily jump up to lick her on the cheek and had the most infectious smile. Georgia helped me climb into the large open tub before she scrubbed me good and hard, especially my tummy, which was my favorite. She laughed as she applied a fresh scent conditioner that I've been told by so many young female guests smells like bubble gum, whatever that is. I don't mind because I get so much attention every time they tell me that. Georgia's touch felt so good I didn't want her to stop. She dried my fur with a blow drier, brushed me, and squeezed my face before planting a huge kiss on each side. No bright red lipstick today. Thank goodness. I licked her cheek, wagged my tail with approval, and shot her one of my irresistible smiles before Nate and I returned to The Inn.

We walked behind the front desk and into his office where he smoothed my fur before he took off my Two Turtles Inn collar and replaced it with a floral patterned one that had a matching silky bowtie. I tilted my head, wondering who was getting married and why I wasn't wearing my Two Turtles Inn tie. I've been here almost four months and introduced many brides and grooms, most needing a second chance at love, who request me to be ring bearer at their weddings, but still I puzzled. Why was today different with a special bow tie and why was it my day as well? Since I had to wait to find out, my mind drifted back to the day Nate adopted me, gave me my second chance at love, and how that love brought me here to The Two Turtles Inn on Sanibel Island, Florida.

———

I'm a very lucky dog. So much so "Lucky" should have been my name. My mom, Goldie, a beautiful smart Golden Lab, gave birth to me in a Florida Service Dog training center. But my birth, no matter how joyful, came with the biggest scandal to ever hit the likes of that facility. Mom became weary of all their rules, a trait I inherited from her and understand more than any other dog I know. At that time, she was in heat. The vet kept her isolated so he could introduce her to the perfect service dog match.

Guess she couldn't wait because she told me, "One sunny day I broke out of my pen. I pawed up the latch, pushed the screen door open, and went for a wonderful free run that ended at the local park. Along the way, I played with every dog I met and loved every minute of it. Once in the park, my heart came to a complete stop when I saw the man of my dreams, a terrier chow mix who stole my heart in an instant. He was playful, handsome, and flirtatious. Still in heat, I fell head over paws in love. Into the bushes we romped where you, along with your seven other siblings, were conceived.

"The staff at the training center combed the different areas of the park, searching for me. They knew how crucial their timing was in locating me. One staffer trainee named Chuck, who wanting to impress his supervisor, combed every scrub until he discovered me with your dad in the bushes and was pleased he could be the first to yell as loud as he could. 'She's here, but I think we might be a little too late.'"

A little too late was an understatement. Anyway, I was told there she was with my dad, whom I've never met, carrying on like a teenage pup. After the staff separated the two love birds, they escorted Mom back to the shelter on a leash. A little over a week later, our vet confirmed she was pregnant. Being a humane animal center, the powers that be let nature take its course.

I was the runt of the litter of eight puppies. The center adopted out my seven brothers and sisters as soon as they were old enough to loving homes for free since none of them met the service dog training qualifications. They all were cute with fluffy red hair and curly tails but had my father's IQ. Unlike my siblings, I, however, inherited my mother's smarts and some of her good golden lab looks mixed in with Dad's chow and terrier.

For that reason, Bruce, a veterinarian who loved all of us, and was head of the center, told me, "Max, I have high hopes for you. I placed you in the service dog program because I observed how curious you were, how sensitive you were to people, not to mention the fact that you inherited Goldie's intelligence."

But even with all those wonderful traits, I had two strikes against me. I considered commands a mere suggestion, and I loved people and other animals so much my feelings for them often clouded my judgement. That, however, did not stop a wonderful middle-aged couple, the Sutherlings, from committing to take me home for one year and teach me the basics of being a service dog.

Having served as one herself, Mom advised me before I left, "Max, you were born to do great things for those who lost their sight and others needing help with handicaps both physical and emotional." I guess I have helped humans at The Inn this past year…just not who and how Mom had intended.

The Sutherlings were gracious, sharing their home to train me while loving me as if I was their own dog. I know that took a special quality of selflessness since they had to return me to the center in one year so I could graduate to the next level of training. Proud to wear my service dog training harness, I knew I was not to be petted or hugged even though I wanted to be ever so badly. I tried as hard as I could to obey those rules but just couldn't.

My dilemma remained constant; I loved people. I loved kids. I loved other dogs and other animals and always wanted to show them how much. No surprise, since like Mom, I was rebellious and ignored any rules that prevented me from showing my love. On training walks, I'd sneak a kiss to the back of passing strangers' hands, hoping they would stop to pet me. In the middle of the night, I'd slip in to visit Harry, the Sutherling's kindhearted youngest son, and sleep on the floor next to his bed so as not to wake him.

My love of humans took over my behavior so much that after eight months of instruction, my training ended abruptly. That nice couple returned me to the service dog facility and addressed my training issues with Bruce. "We feel Max doesn't want to be trained; he'd rather love and be loved. We've tried repeatedly to change his attitude and behavior, but to no avail, so with heavy hearts, we are returning him to you."

Bruce, a human teddy bear, gave me one more shot to train on campus. He tried as hard as he could but found that I'm a people dog through and through. One Saturday morning, Bruce took my trainer Megan, a fun, energetic, twenty-two-year-old, and me into his office, where instructed me to sit. I did that easily but was not prepared for what was to come next. Bruce rubbed his fuzzy beard before looking me in the eyes and saying the words I hoped never to hear. He spoke to me slowly as if he thought I could understand Human.

"Max, you're not going to make it as a sight or any kind of service dog, but don't get discouraged. This isn't your fault. Somewhere in this big wide world, a job is waiting for your special skills. I've placed you in our adoption program and will be extra careful to select the right forever parents for you."

After my trainer left me with Bruce, I plopped down on the rug in his office and put my head on my paws, thinking, "How will Mom feel when she learns I flunked out? She had such high hopes for me."

By the frown on his face, I could tell Bruce knew his decision depressed me, but as I was soon to find out, Bruce kept his word. He was very particular about my adoptive parents and, as Megan informed me, one of our daily walks, "Rest easy Max. So far, Bruce has already turned down three prospective parents. He wants to find the right ones."

Then one sunny Monday morning, Megan came bounding into my pen and in a very cheerful voice said, "Come with me Max, Bruce wants to see you." As soon as we entered Bruce's office, I noticed a kind looking man in his mid-thirties standing next to Bruce's large oak desk. Megan stroked my head before she leaned down and whispered in my ear, "Maxie, look how his kind blue eyes sparkle when he looks at you. He's tan, blond, and ever so handsome. If you weren't my main man, I sure could go for him."

That tall, well-dressed man walked over to pet me. My tail wagged a mile a minute as I sat up straight as an arrow and handed him my paw. Couldn't help it, I wanted a forever home more than anything else in my doggy world. Bruce then spoke to me in Human again. I liked that much better than puppy talk. "Max, you were our featured adoptee of the month and this caring man, a long-time friend of mine, Nate Pierson, answered the call. Nate and I attended the University of Florida together. We haven't connected in a few years, so you can imagine how surprised I was when he inquired about adopting you..."

I looked up to see Megan smiling from ear to ear as she gave me a thumbs up. Maybe Bruce really did find my next pet parent? This gentle looking soul took my bait, hook, line, and sinker because he smiled and said, "Hey Max, I'm Nate and I have a good feeling you may be just what we need." We? That puzzled me enough to tilt my head. Does he have a family? A wife? Bruce looked at me, feeling the need to explain again in Human. Since I'm a dog, Bruce isn't sure how much I understand. Humans can be so funny. For some reason, they don't understand, I think of them as just another species of animals.

"Max and Megan, I'd like you to introduce you to Nate Pierson who owns The Two Turtles Inn on Sanibel Island. He's looking for a buddy, not only for himself but one to share with his guests and give them comfort and help with their exercise. He called yesterday after seeing your photo on our website and wanted to know all about you."

Nate looking straight down into my eyes and said the magic words I waited what seemed like forever to hear. "I'm looking for a dog to share my home and life, that loves everyone, doesn't have a mean bone in his body, and is smart and knows commands. Bruce already advised me that you knew all kinds of commands but did not always obey them."

Both men laughed as Nate knelt next to me. "Bruce, just spending these few minutes with Max, I know he's the perfect fit for me and The Inn. I can't wait to have fun with him and give him the love he deserves. I was inspired to find a dog I could share with my guests after reading an article about a canine concierge serving one of the larger chain hotels in downtown Chicago. That dog was not available for walks but in room supervised visits with guests. Our inn sits on a beautiful Gulf Coast Island and has many walking paths and a gorgeous beach awaiting Max to share with our guests, but I can't lie. I'm excited he's coming home to be my dog. I'll take the best care of him. I want to thank you, so besides writing a check for the normal adoption fee, I'm adding a five-hundred-dollar donation."

I wagged my tail. I must have charmed him beyond measure.

Bruce smiled as Nate wrote the check. "We're truly grateful. Your generosity will help with our training mission. Nate, I appreciate this personally since we're friends."

They shook hands, after which Bruce took off my training collar with the school's logo embroidered on it and replaced it with a plain collar before handing Nate my leash. He looked at me with tears in his eye. "Max, my buddy, I'll miss you. Have a great life. You deserve it."

As Nate walked me out of Bruce's office, I couldn't look back thinking about leaving Bruce, Megan, Mom who remained at the center a little longer than usual to train with her new pet parent, a little girl named Shirley who was wheelchair bound, and all the rest of my friends. I was happy to find a forever home, but sad knowing I'd never see any of them again. We walked to Nate's dark-colored pick-up truck with Turtle Inn signs on both doors and I hopped onto the passenger seat, my tail wagging so fast it wouldn't stop. Nate fastened a harness around me. "Okay buddy, you're ready to roll. I'm not going to change your name. Max has a nice ring to it."

He leaned in and gave me a hug. "I want you to know I'll always be here for you."

I thumped my tail on the seat, happy to hear him say that before he asked, "Ready to go home?"

Was I ever ready! Home...that word sounded so good, and I was so eager for one. Nate started the truck, and we were off in a flash. Our ride was long, but beautiful. The training center was in the middle of the state; The Inn on the Southwest Gulf Coast of Florida.

After a while, we headed over a long bridge to a beautiful, sun-swept island with loads of greenery and large homes. Nate rolled down my window so I could stick my nose out to smell the salt water and feel the cool sea breezes. Everything looked and smelled so fresh, like my own fresh start in life.

Nate called someone from his cell. "Wendy, I have him. His name's Max and everyone's going to fall in love with him the minute they meet him. See you in about ten minutes."

We continued down the tree-lined main street before Nate slowed down and pointed to a sign. "Here we are Max. Your new home ...The Two Turtles Inn."

He winked. "You're going to adore it here, pal. There's a wide, soft, sandy beach right across the street and we have some docks in the Back Bay for boats. Our lawn is big and fun for play and walks on special paths."

I loved the kind way Nate spoke to me. As we turned into the long pebble driveway, I saw six young people all in matching shirts with a turtle on the pocket lined up waiting for us. As we approached, they applauded. Nate beamed. "Okay, Max, let's meet the other members of your family."

Three excited young women, all in their early twenties, wearing turtle shirts and matching green shorts, ran over to our truck and opened my door. I hopped out to be surrounded with hugs and kisses. Honestly, never in my life have I been this happy.

Three young men followed. I sat up straight and held out my paw as one remarked. "He's great. I can't wait to take him for a walk."

I still had on my leash, but nobody held onto it. I know I could have run off but why would I? This place was amazing. I heard Nate's truck door close before he walked over to me. "Come on, buddy, let's go inside."

We walked to the entrance of this lovely old southern mansion with clapboard shutters and a large two-story addition on the left side. I happily pranced up the ten stairs to a big porch with wicker rockers filled with guests. As Nate walked me over to meet each of them, my tail wagged so hard I feared it would fall off.

"Good boy." Nate gave me a quick pat. "Bruce was right. You really do love people. Now let's go inside and see your new home."

After meeting all those wonderful people, we walked inside. I wondered if I was in a royal palace. I looked up to see a stunning palm-shaped, rattan ceiling fan. My eyes then caught a glimpse of a large seating area under two tall indoor palms that faced floor to ceiling windows over-looking the beach, a far cry from my view at the training center. A pleasant looking woman dressed in The Inn's uniform stood behind a tall desk and smiled as Nate introduced us. She looked about his age, was pretty in a natural way, with a friendly smile, dark hair, and kind dark eyes.

"Wendy, please come and meet our newest team member, Max." Nate knelt and petted me. "Wendy Abbot supervises our front desk and is The Inn's assistant manager. You'll be spending a great deal of time out here with her."

Wendy immediately ran out from behind the front desk, excited to greet me. She gave me a big hug and kissed the top of my head. I fell in love with her at once. Who wouldn't after such a wonderful greeting? Better yet, she smelled like the wildflowers behind the shelter I liked to sniff. "Maxie, Nate told me he was going to adopt a friendly dog for The Inn, but you're more magnificent than I ever could have imagined. We're going to have fun getting to know each other. We're all happy to welcome you to your new home. Come with me."

I walked with her around the front desk to discover a natural wicker bed holding the fluffiest pillow I ever saw with a sign across the front. Wendy pointed to it. "This is for you, Max. Our new Canine Concierge. You are official just as that sign says."

I was so happy I spun around chasing my tail until I became dizzy. A home and a job! Everyone in the lobby watched and laughed, but I had a new job and couldn't wait to get started.

It wasn't five minutes later when the large double oak front doors opened. In came a tall, muscular, good-looking man. I could sense by his demeanor, he was down in the mouth. Aha, I bet he could use a little Max time.

Wendy instructed me to stay. I did exactly as she said because my new bed was so soft and comfy. She walked around the desk and shook the man's hand. "Dr. Aaron Swift. It's my pleasure to welcome you back to The Inn. Congratulations on your wedding. Our entire staff wants to make your honeymoon as memorable as possible."

Dr. Swift was silent as Wendy continued. "How was the

drive from Florida's lovely East Coast, in particular Boca Raton?"

From my vantage point, I saw Dr. Aaron put his head down and shuffle his feet when Wendy asked. "May I send our bell captain to assist the new Mrs. Swift with her bags?"

I watched the doctor cover his eyes with his hands and I couldn't help myself. Something was wrong, so I disobeyed Wendy's command, stood up, walked over to him, and rubbed my head against his leg. I sensed Wendy thought a great deal of Dr. Swift, who leaned down to pet me the minute he saw me.

She immediately instructed me, "Max, please go back to your bed." Turning to the doctor, she said, "I apologize for Max's behavior. It's his first day as our canine concierge."

Finally, a smile appeared on Dr. Swift's face as he continued to pet me. "It's quite all right, Wendy. He's a good boy."

I decided I should stay by his side. He looked down at me. "I can tell you're a buddy. You remind me of Buster, the dog I had growing up. He was a mixed breed as well."

The doctor's eyes filled with tears as he looked up and said, "Wendy, there was no wedding. Beth broke our engagement four weeks before we were to be married. Our wedding day broken, so was my heart. I had already booked and paid The Inn for our honeymoon and since it was too late to cancel, I decided I needed to take a vacation, an emotional break, from work, stress, and my broken heart."

I looked over at Wendy, who was speechless. I could tell she didn't know how to respond, so she began telling the doctor about me. "Please allow me to properly introduce you to Max. He's the newest member of our resort staff and, as I already told you, our canine concierge. Max has a wonderful, comforting way about him. Doesn't he? We adopted him after he completed six months of service dog training. He loves people. He's such a great listener and so caring, I've decided to nickname him 'my furball of love'."

I liked Wendy's nickname for me and hoped to live up to it. Dr. Swift must have liked it too, because he smiled and stroked me again. "Max is a furball of love. He sure knows how to soothe a person."

Wendy continued. "Today is his first day here. We need to do a bit more training, but he'll be available for walks in two days on Wednesday, starting at 10:00 a.m. If you'd like to sign up, I've already started a page in his appointment book, and you'll be the first walk on his schedule."

Aaron Swift looked at me and chuckled. "Max, you must be pretty important to have your own schedule. It's been a long time since I had a dog. Your first walk as concierge … I'm honored. Max, I think you may be just what I need."

I tilted my head even though I already knew he was right. Once I'm trained, I'll do my best to make everyone happy. While Doctor Swift signed up for his 10 a.m. walk, Wendy called for the bell captain to get the doctor's luggage and escort him to his room. He patted my head one more time before leaving.

Dr. Aaron's broken heart... I'm sure I can find a fix for that. As I watched him leave, I heard those double front doors open again.

CHAPTER
TWO

After two days of pretending to learn things I already knew, like not to jump on people and how to follow a person's pace when walking, I was bored but anxious to get started on my first day as concierge. Early this morning after breakfast, Nate took me to the spa where my groomer, Georgia, prepared me for my big day. She was so different, so much gentler than my handlers at the training center who washed me in a large metal tub and used a bristled scrub brush at the end of a long wooden handle. Georgia wore soft gloves and scrubbed me with her hands.

Once Georgia was pleased that I looked my best, she walked me back to the front lobby where Wendy finished my special appearance by fastening a new collar with the swimming turtles from The Two Turtles Inn logo around my neck before snapping a coordinating bow tie to it. I now matched her uniform and almost everything else I could see. Outfit complete, Wendy squeezed my cheeks and gushed. Why does everyone love to squeeze my cheeks? Guess I'm too cute for words.

"Look at you, Max. Emerald-green and white are your

colors. They highlight your gorgeous golden brown and red fur."

Since I'm color challenged, all dogs are, I felt good hearing that from Wendy. Maybe I'll be able to help Aaron, the good doctor, if he tells me more about himself. He seemed like a great guy, someone I'd like to know better, so I'm sure someone else would too.

Wendy became excited. "It's 10:00 a.m. Time for your very first walk with a guest. Are you ready to go to work?" I wagged my tail like crazy as I watched that elevator door open. Wow! It was Dr. Swift. He was prompt...to the minute.

Dr. Swift, sporting madras shorts and a Miami Hurricanes T-shirt, blurted out before he even reached the front desk. "Hey Wendy, Max looks great. I can't wait for our walk."

Wendy fastened my leash to the collar and handed one end to the doctor. Aaron Swift grinned as he looked down at me. "Max, ready? Let's boogey." Boogey is what he wanted, so out the front door I scampered as he hung on from behind. From the porch I could see The Inn's massive front lawn that faced the Gulf of Mexico. I knew he'd enjoy the walking paths I'd practiced on for the last two days because they had so many colorful shrubs, beautiful water views, and fragrant flowers awaiting us.

First, we walked by guests playing Frisbee and lawn darts to reach the path I selected for him with expansive views of the Back Bay. This particular path had uneven ground, what with all the pebbles on it, so I took it slow, not knowing how fit the doctor was. He surprised me by walking at a brisk pace. About fifteen minutes into our walk, Aaron found and sat on a park bench. He didn't appear to be winded or aching, so I sat in front of him, placing my head on his knees and looking up into his eyes.

Tears rolled down his cheeks as he began to talk to me. "Max, I know I need to talk to someone about this and you seem like the perfect listener because you can't talk back. My head's burdened with guilt while my heart's broken into a million pieces."

I tilted my head and picked up my ears.

"I thought I was going to get married last Saturday. Everything was set from the church to the reception, to the dresses and tuxes. Then about four weeks ago, the love of my life, Beth, broke off our engagement over dinner and handed me back this."

He paused to reach into his shorts' pocket and pull out a small velvet box. He opened the box to reveal a sparking engagement ring. I rubbed his knee with my furry head so he knew I understood.

"I carry her ring with me, hoping she'll call and tell me she made a mistake and wants me back. I'd be so happy I'd arrange the wedding of her dreams all over again on the spot. You know, Maxie, we were together for six years."

I continued to listen to Aaron, who, overcome by his sadness, put his head in his hands. I licked them and wagged my tail, hoping to give him some encouragement.

"Can you believe it, buddy? I brought my tux in case she called and changed her mind. We don't need a big fancy ceremony, just a wedding. I've left several messages telling her I was here and still loved her and forgave her, but so far have not received a response. I try at least once every day. Maybe one of my messages will break through that icy atmosphere she created between us."

Just then, in typical Florida style, the clouds burst open, catching us in a cooling shower.

Aaron put the ring back in his pocket, stood, and pulled his T-shirt over his head, trying to protect himself from getting wet. I stood and followed him, running back to The Inn. We ran up the front steps as fast as we could, hoping to find Wendy. She was there waiting, holding two large pool towels ready to dry us off. We were both soaked. I must have looked pretty funny because Aaron looked at me and couldn't stop laughing. "Max, you look like a drowned rat. Can't even imagine how bad I must look. I haven't had this much fun since I was a kid. Wendy, since we still have a little time left, we'll sit on the front porch and watch the rain."

Wendy, worried about our drenched clothes, raced to get more towels from the housekeeping closet. She brought them out to us on the porch. Aaron dried me off first. That's what I love about humans. Wendy took one look at me and shook her head. "Max, after all that grooming…"

Aaron took the second towel and dried himself. He must have really enjoyed our walk because he asked Wendy, "I'd like to book Max for a walk every day I'm here at the same time, please. He's one great pal. I'll stop by the front desk on my way up to my room to confirm this. For now, we'll sit on the porch until our time together is up."

We sat there silently, watching the rain fall into the Gulf. Aaron hugged me when our time was up, and we returned to Wendy. She had the appointment book, now with my enlarged photo on the cover, out on the counter and looked at the schedule.

"Since this is Max's first day, I have this same time available every day during your stay with us. I'll block those times and print out your appointments. Max will be getting quite popular as more guests meet him, so you are wise to book future walks with him today."

Wendy made me sound like a rock star. Why wasn't I surprised? I don't want to brag, but I was the most popular pup for hugging at the training center.

Aaron petted my head and said, "Thanks Wendy. See you tomorrow, Maxie." His printed appointment sheet in hand, he headed for the elevator.

Lucky for me, the Forrest twins, also known as the terrible twosome, showed up late for their first walk with me, so Wendy had extra time to towel dry me and change my collar, bow tie, and leash.

As soon as they arrived, Mrs. Forrest, a tall slender woman with dark curly hair, told Wendy, "We're so excited. It stopped raining, and the sun is out, so we could keep our appointment. If the twins behave with Max, we might be able to get a dog of our own once we get home."

Ouch! The first thing those two little terrors did was to grab my tail and pull it. Wendy, firm, stepped in at once. "Boys, cut that out. If that's how you'll treat our Max, you may not take him for a walk. That's the rule. "

Mrs. Forrest, miffed at her two boys, added, "That's right. You must respect him. Wendy, I will walk Max. The boys will follow."

Wendy looked reluctant. I can't say I blame her. Oh me, oh my, what will I do if they get rambunctious? I was trained not to respond with aggression or bite, only to help and show love. I saw Wendy shoot a quick wink to Mathew, one of our groundskeepers who took me on a training walk yesterday. I've been told by some of the female staff that he's very handsome. By the smile on Wendy's face, I'm sure she thinks so too. Mathew was on a coffee break, so he put his coffee mug down on an outside table and nodded to show Wendy he understood.

Wendy, appearing calmer, handed Mrs. Forrest my

leash. Off we went down the steps as I led them onto one of the easier walking paths. Mathew followed, carrying a rake and a bottle of water to work in the same area where we walked. Bobby Forrest, a chubby kid with freckles, stomped his feet and started to speak in his snarly kid voice. "Mama, I want to walk Max." Bret, the larger of the twins and a carbon copy of Bobby just without the freckles, pushed him aside. "No, let me". Thank goodness Mrs. Forrest held firm. "When you respect Max, you can walk him."

Looking back, I saw Mathew still following at a safe distance behind us. We, or should I say I, finished the small walking path without incident. Mrs. Forrest looked at her watch before leading us back to the front desk with the twins still whining about not holding my leash. Just as we arrived at the front entrance, a fancy, bright colored sports car pulled into the front entrance portico.

The car stopped. The bellman approached as the driver popped the trunk open from inside the car. Wow, three large suitcases...must be either for a big group or an extra-long stay. Then only one person exited the car; a beautiful, well-dressed woman with dark hair emerged. Wish I was closer and without the twins, so I could sniff her when she petted me. Women always do, and I enjoyed feeling the softness of their touch.

When I finished my walk with the Forrest family, we all returned to the front desk. Mrs. Forrest advised Wendy. "The boys are not allowed near Max until they can behave." She handed Wendy my leash. "However, I'll call to schedule a walk with him again in a couple of days after I instruct the boys on how to treat a pet."

Wendy smiled and nodded her approval to Mrs. Forrest before the three left for their rooms. I turned as Wendy unfastened my leash to see that woman I saw outside make her way to the check-in desk. The bellman followed with a cart overloaded with stuff.

Wendy greeted the new arrival with a big smile. "You must be Stephanie Jakes. Love your bright blue sports car. Did it rain much on the way down from Tampa?"

Stephanie laughed. Her dark eyes sparkled. "You bet it did almost all the way down. It started to clear about an hour ago. My car didn't miss one drop. How else would the weather be on the first day of my vacation?"

Wendy interjected, "You'll be happy to know your room is ready, but I need to check you in before I can give you a key and have your luggage sent up."

Stephanie brushed her long, dark hair aside and looked down at me. "Poor guy, he's a cutie but looks like he's been through the mill."

Wendy explained. "He just experienced meeting some energetic twins but luckily their mom kept them at bay during their walk with our Max." Wendy added, "Thank goodness she took charge. Hopefully, those young boys will leave here with a better respect for animals and know not to treat them like stuffed toys to throw around."

Stephanie looked surprised. "Walk? Is this something new?"

Wendy replied, "Why yes, it is. We have a new staff member at The Two Turtles Inn and walks are his specialty."

Stephanie clapped her hands. "How wonderful is that? Last time I was here with my ex-husband, we were taking a break from his Senate race and this handsome young man was not available."

Wendy looked sad. "I was so sorry to read about your divorce. They can be so stressful especially when they're in the public eye."

Stephanie laughed. "Not mine. Glad to rid myself of that bossy man. Now I'm free to do as I please. I loved The Inn when we stayed here and came back to unwind before I go back to work at my former advertising firm. I remember how wonderful your spa was and can't wait to make an appointment. Now please introduce me to your newest and cutest staff member."

That was my cue to sit up as straight as an arrow and wag my tail. Of course, I gave her my best puppy dog stare. Wendy then formally introduced us. "Stephanie Jakes, please meet Max our canine concierge. He's available for walks or just to sit with on the porch or if you feel energetic to play Frisbee or tennis ball. Max is eight and a half months old and has had service dog training for six months. We're so lucky to have him. When he's not on duty, he goes home with Nate, our owner, who is his pet parent."

Stephanie smiled as she stroked my back. "I'd love to sit with Max this afternoon on a lawn chair, if that's possible. I drove almost four hours in the rain to get here and since the sun is peeking through the clouds, I could use a brief break before settling into my room."

Wendy took out my appointment book and opened it to check my schedule.

Stephanie gushed at my photo on the cover. "What a great photo. Max you're very photogenic."

That's right. I know how handsome I am. Wendy paid no attention to my tail wagging and continued. "Max will be available for photos with our adult guests tomorrow morning from eight to nine a.m. on our front steps. Of course, there is a charge, but all monies from the photo shoot will be donated to our local animal shelter. He is available at three today for a sit. If the weather doesn't stay clear, you can sit on our porch. Would you like me to schedule that?"

"Yes, of course. I'm here for two weeks, so when I'm rid of my dark circles, I'll arrange for a photo as well. Max, you'll look great on my desk." Stephanie passed a credit card to Wendy, who finished checking Stephanie in before handing her a key.

"See you at three, Max. Maybe when I go into the village to those wonderful craft shops, I'll find Max some treats. Last time I was here, there was a doggy bakery in the village."

A doggy bakery! My tail wagged a mile a minute. I've never eaten any cookies from a doggy bakery. Sounds real good to me. Stephanie quickly became my new favorite guest. I wondered what other surprises she had in store for me at three o'clock. Will I be able to go to the doggy bakery with her?

CHAPTER
THREE

I t was almost three. Can't lie, I was so tired from greeting guests, being petted, and taking those twins for a walk, I would have loved to stay on my soft pillow bed and take a nap. That was, until I heard Stephanie's voice in the lobby.

"Catherine, what a wonderful surprise! Fancy meeting you here. I have a three o'clock appointment but would love to catch up. Maybe tea at four-thirty? Sounds great. That's a date. Meet you in the coffee shop. Gotta run."

I watched Stephanie vigorously walk to the front desk. "Hi Wendy, I'm here on time, an amazing feat for me, for my three o'clock with Max. I just ran into my former college roommate whom I haven't seen in two years since our tenth reunion. I'm going to meet her later. Now, more importantly, how's my boy?"

I stretched, got up, and walked over to her. I nudged her leg. Stephanie's so soft and smells so good, like roses from The Inn's garden. I nuzzled until she knelt to hug me.

"Max, the guests are lucky you're here. You would have made an excellent therapy dog. We're going to have fun today getting to know each other better and again soon on our first real walk."

Wendy fastened my leash and handed it to Stephanie. We headed out the front door and down the steps before stopping at the bottom for a few minutes to check out the sky. It had stopped raining, and the sun was out. Stephanie perused the area, deciding the best place for us to go. We scooted by the Forrest twins playing Frisbee, hoping to avoid them, but we weren't fast enough because they spotted us and shouted, "Hey, there's Max. Let's go say hello."

I jumped behind Stephanie, who was quick to catch on. She turned to confront them. "No can do, boys. I've got him for the hour, so keep on playing."

She quick turned toward a walking path and we made a beeline for the bushes that lined both sides of it. Once we were out of their sight, Stephanie laughed so hard she doubled over. "Max, I haven't had this much fun in years. Those two look like little monsters."

There was a park bench about five yards from us, so Stephanie walked us there and sat down. "I didn't expect to jog after all the driving I did to get here especially in the pouring rain. Max, we're going to relax and get to know each other." She took a deep breath. "I'm so happy to be here and not working on a Senate race. I would love to have a pet like you, but I work way too many hours to be able to take good care of one."

I dropped down by her feet to lie on the lush moist grass as she petted my head. The wind blew softly across the shrubs. She wore a flowered backpack, which she removed. She opened it, took out a bottle of water and two paper cups. "Max, you and I are going to toast the beginning of a wonderful friendship. Hope the next two weeks are happy for both of us. Right now, you're the only man I want in my life."

Didn't expect to hear that. That made me wonder what the other men in her life were like, but since I don't speak Human, I couldn't ask who or why. I slurped water from the paper cup as she drank hers. She surprised me by taking out a plastic bag filled with carrot sticks. "I love carrots. I eat so many I think I could be part rabbit." She laughed. "All kidding aside, a vet I knew and dated, I might add, a long time ago told me dogs love carrots too. Besides, they're good for both of us, so you enjoy the first one."

I had been trained not to take food from a stranger without my handler's consent, but Stephanie? I never had carrots before. Nate ate them all the time. I didn't want to disappoint her, so I gently took one from her hand and crunched on it like a rawhide stick while she chewed on hers. Hmmm. Carrot sticks were much softer and much sweeter. I could learn to like these. Wonder if we'll have some tomorrow?

Stephanie glanced at her watch. "I'm returning to work for my former employer, a large marketing and public relations firm in Tampa. I'm dedicated and good at what I do, so I've always been in high demand. I work long hours and try to meet my customers' needs. The money's great, but my personal life suffered. I gave my job up a short while ago to marry my last client. He swept me off my feet. You know that old saying 'love at first sight.' But more about that on our next walk."

I couldn't wait. I'm sure glad I understood Human because Stephanie really enjoyed talking to me. She stood. "Time flies with a handsome dude like you. Think we'd better head back before Wendy sends out a search and rescue team to find us. We still have a little time left, so we'll take our time. I'll have to cancel tomorrow's walk because of a hair appointment in town. Maybe I can find that doggy bakery while I'm there, but I promise that will be my only cancellation."

I buried my head in my paws to show her just how dejected that made me. Stephanie smiled and petted my head. "Don't worry Maxie, we'll be spending so much time together, you'll tire of me." I doubted that. Her comment made me so happy my tail wagged all the way back to the front lobby and Wendy. I couldn't wait to be with her again, curious to learn more about this beautiful but mysterious woman's past and why I was the only man she wanted in her life.

CHAPTER
FOUR

After two great walks and one menacing one with the Forrest twins, I was beat and couldn't wait for Nate to take me upstairs to our apartment and tuck me in. My first day on the job; three outings and I was so tired I didn't even feel like eating.

Nate came out of his office happy to see me and took me up to our cozy apartment. He always tried to take the best care of me and made my dinner of healthy dog food. He placed my bowl in front of me, but I just stared at it. He puzzled at my lack of appetite. "Max, are you feeling okay? I'm used to you wolfing down dinner."

I ate some but pushed the rest aside in my dish to make my portion look smaller so he wouldn't worry. It must have worked, because we went into our small living room. Ready to snuggle next to him on the couch, Nate, a known workaholic, wasn't ready for that just yet. He wanted to teach me a couple of new tricks to prepare for my debut magic show for our youngest guests. I was tired but loved Nate so much I didn't want to disappoint him. Besides I saw him take a box of cookies from the kitchen cabinet. As Mom said, "There's always room for cookies."

"Tonight," he began, "we're going to learn the brown cookie white cookie trick and also a trick called the flying cookieendas."

Anything with cookies sounded good to me. I've always been a quick study and enjoyed "brown cookie-white cookie" because I got to eat the ones I identified correctly. The flying cookiendas was a bit tougher. Nate stood and held a cookie way up in the air. I had to catch it while seated with my mouth wide open. That trick took more time to perfect. Nate looked happy after my first lesson but tired soon afterwards. I can see him in his office from my concierge bed in the lobby and know how hard he works. "Okay, buddy, we'll practice these tricks every day until your show. The kids are going to love it. Now, let's watch TV."

I couldn't wait. The program was an exciting western, but we both soon fell asleep. I thought I heard Nate get up but was so groggy my head fell back down on the throw pillow, and I went back to sleep. The next morning, I woke up in the same position on the couch, covered with a light quilt. Nate must have covered me before he left for bed. Unlike last night, I woke up famished and tackled my breakfast like a tiger. Nate looked at his watch. "We're late. It's seven. I'll get your bow tie."

All set, we came inside from my brief walk to find Wendy at the front desk checking in new guests. I greeted each one of them, tail wagging. She laughed. "It's about time you two sleepyheads arrived. I was concerned Max would be late for his portraits with our adult guests and afterwards, his first walk of the day."

I knew Aaron was my first walk and couldn't wait. Time

flew as I heard the camera click what seemed like a million times. Of course, after each portrait, I received hugs from that guest. Portraits over and back to my post, I watched Aaron step out of the elevator. He wore plaid shorts and a Two Turtles Inn T-shirt. Excited to get going, I wanted to learn more about this nice guy.

"Good morning, Wendy. And how's my best bud, Max? Ready for our jaunt, pal?"

Wendy handed Aaron my leash, and we walked down the steps to the lawn and the walking path. For some reason, he looked happier today. Maybe that Max time yesterday did him some good. We walked a bit further down the same path we took yesterday until we found a park bench farther away from The Inn. Aaron sat on the bench. I surprised him and jumped up to sit next to him which made him laugh.

"Max, you're the best." He smiled, ruffling my fur. "I need to tell you more about my planned wedding so I can get that sad story off my chest. Beth and I met a little over six years ago. I was in my last year of residency training to be a gynecologist. I fell hard for her at first sight. She was and still is the most beautiful woman I ever met with her green eyes and shoulder length red hair. We shared similar life views, laughed at the same jokes, and liked the same restaurants. We even finished each other's sentences. We were a match made in heaven."

Aaron paused. "So almost five years later, to the date, I took her to Orlando for a long weekend and proposed in front of Cinderella's castle. As I got down on one knee, I could hear a zillion cameras snapping behind me. I brought that beautiful emerald and diamond ring I showed you to give her if she said 'yes'. Emeralds are her favorite.

"Her quick response took me by complete surprise

because she knew what she was getting into. As a gynecologist, I was always on call. Babies don't make appointments. During all this time, she thought it was wonderful I went into women's health, so she, more than anyone, knew who I was and what I did."

He sighed. "But I had prepared for a 'yes' and arranged to have our engagement photos taken the next day on the park's antique carousel. She adored those photos and after she selected her favorite one, we sent out announcements."

Aaron stopped to take a deep breath, I'm sure to collect his thoughts. "So, you can see how her decision to break off our engagement took me by complete surprise. She said I was a 'workaholic' and not who she wanted in a husband. She came to this decision a little more than four weeks ago. I did have erratic hours, but as I already said, babies do not wait. I guess my schedule finally got to her. For love's sake, we spent six years together, but as she told me, 'I worried there would be little time in our lives for each other, never mind kids, family trips, or even pets. Even pets, imagine that?'"

That last statement was especially hard for me to swallow. Who wouldn't have time for a pet? We're so lovable, I thought, as he resumed his story.

"Why didn't she complain five years ago when I first opened my practice?" Aaron continued. "She knew how much I loved her and how much she meant to me. I can't wrap my head around this whole thing. This vacation was supposed to be our honeymoon. We had stayed at The Inn before when I could only squeeze an overnight getaway into my schedule and we both loved it so much that we chose it over any other place in the world for our honeymoon. I'd already arranged for another doctor to cover me for the two weeks I'd be gone."

Aaron wiped his eyes. "I promised her after she called off our wedding that I would try to work less, maybe take in another partner, but she wasn't convinced. She said I had plenty of time to do that already. She told me, 'You would say or do anything to keep us together.' She sounded so cold and distant, I got the feeling she met someone else. I had never seen her like that before. I was always the center of her universe, as she was of mine."

Aaron started to cry. "When I suspected there might be someone else, I enlisted the help of my best man, Stuart, to find out who that might be."

He pounded his fist on his knee. "Guess what Max? After I asked him, Stuart, my ex-college roommate, and best friend, said he couldn't lie to me any longer. He said Beth might be able to, but he couldn't. Stu then admitted he was the other man. His betrayal pierced my heart like a dagger. He told me, 'Beth became depressed because you left her alone so many nights and weekends. She confided in me, wondering if that's what her married life would be like. At first, I tried to comfort her telling her what a wonderful guy you were, but my comfort turned into something else. We fell for each other and started dating. We're both very happy.'"

I looked at Aaron, who shook his head in disbelief. "'Both very happy', isn't that swell? Well, what about me? Did you know her parents couldn't afford her dream wedding? I paid for anything and everything she wanted, so our special day would be perfect. If any good came out of this mess, it's that four weeks was enough time to get most of my deposits back, but I'd be willing to lose every penny of that money if she would come back to me. I'd pay for everything all over again. If she'd reconsider, I'd take her back in a second. I never realized how much I hurt her."

Aaron stroked my head, helping him calm down. "Enough with my troubles. Max, you sure are the best listener. Anyway, it felt good to get that all off my chest. I've had my feelings about Stu and Beth bottled up since I found out about them. Our break- up and cancelled wedding was bad enough."

I snuggled my head in his hand. Aaron looked down at my furry face as I gave him my most endearing look, making him smile.

"Say, Max, let's get back to our walk. I feel better now. I know I'm going to enjoy our daily walks." He stood and we continued around the garden bursting with colorful tropical flowers, then down to the beach road before turning around and heading back to The Inn.

Wendy waved to us from the front porch. She seemed relieved to see us. We walked up the steps and Aaron petted my head before handing Wendy my leash. "Spending more time with Max will make my stay great! He's a fantastic listener."

Wendy smiled. "Thanks Dr. Swift. We all feel that way about him." Aaron thanked Wendy and left to go back to his room. She looked at me. "Come on, Maxie. Let's get ready for your next walk with Mr. and Mrs. Guyer at 11:30."

CHAPTER
FIVE

A very sweet couple, Mr. and Mrs. Guyer, showed up right on time. By their slim stature, white hair, and the slowness of their pace, I knew they were elderly. I overheard Wendy mention to Nate, they were both in their eighties. I remembered from my training, I needed to take it nice and slow and keep them centered on an easy walking path.

Mr. Guyer took one look at me with a twinkle in his eyes and laughed, "Max, you're a beauty. It seems like just yesterday we had Spencer, our beautiful chocolate lab. He and I played tennis ball every day. Does Max like to play?"

Wendy nodded. "He sure does, but you must be careful. He has so much energy, he'll wear you out." She held my tennis ball in her hand to show him.

"Nice bright color. Lime green. Hard for me to miss. Okay, I promise I'll take it easy," he said as he snatched the ball from Wendy's hand. "Max and Anna, we are ready, so off we go."

Anna walked a little slower than her husband, so she held onto his arm. The three of us proceeded down the ramp to an open space a good distance away from all the guests sitting in lounge chairs catching some sun or reading. Mrs. Guyer, still beautiful at her age with delicate facial features and kind eyes, glanced at her husband and winked. "Fred, you're not really going to throw that ball with your bad shoulder, are you?"

Fred, slightly taller than Anna and bald, laughed. "It'll be all right. Maybe I can loosen up some of my arthritis this way. It's like swirling that arm in the air at physical therapy. Max, you ready?'

Was I ready? You bet. Just the sight of that bright colored tennis ball made my ears shoot up and my tail wag so hard I could have spun myself into outer space. Fred held it tight in his hand, so I focused on his every movement. He wound up his arm like a baseball pitcher and was just about to throw the ball when he dropped it and fell to the ground, grabbing his chest.

Anna frantically called out to him, "Fred, are you all right? What's wrong?"

Fred did not respond, so she dropped down next to him beside herself with worry after seeing her husband holding his chest and writhing in such extreme pain. Since no-one was holding onto my leash and we weren't far from the lobby, I raced back up the stairs and barked as loud and as persistently as I could.

By now, I panicked. Fred was in trouble, and I needed to help him.

Wendy rushed out to the front porch. Surprised to see me standing in front of her, she asked, "Max, what's wrong?"

I turned around and barked in Fred and Anna's direction. Wendy looked out at the lawn and saw Fred lying there, grasping his chest as Anna knelt by his side. She immediately took her cell out of her uniform pocket and called the local paramedics. "In the meantime, Max, I'll text Mathew who's working nearby on the grounds and trained in CPR to come give Mr. Guyer immediate assistance."

Since the paramedics had to come from the fire station, I knew Mathew was our best hope to respond in minutes. I looked out still barking as Mathew raced to Fred.

"Wendy, I'll start CPR and do whatever I can to help but we need the assistance of the paramedics. I think he may be having a heart attack." Mathew relayed that through his cell.

Wendy sprinted down the staircase just as the paramedics arrived. They'd arrived faster than usual considering I knew they had to fight beach traffic to get to us. She looked at me. "Max, take Red and Steve to Fred."

I dashed onto the lawn and with Steve, one of the paramedics, hot on my heels, headed for the spot where I left Fred and Anna. Red remained in the ambulance and followed us cautiously. Anna still knelt over her husband as Mathew continued CPR. Our local paramedics did not waste one second. Mathew stepped aside as I watched Red and Steve examine Fred, I realized I had seen them before in Wendy's office. Not in person, but on Wendy's wall.

She could tell by the way I tilted my head at her bulletin board that I wanted to know more about their photos. She shot me a smile. "Our brave and I might add handsome firemen and paramedics do a calendar every year for us islanders. Whatever funds are raised from the sale go to help our local rec center." I think she likes Red a little better than Steve because she tore his page out and pinned it to her bulletin board next to the calendar. Her secret's safe with me. I'll never tell Steve about that.

Steve checked Fred's heart before taking his blood pressure. "His heart's fine. His pulse and blood pressure are stable. We'll take him to the hospital so they can run some tests and determine what's wrong. He's in a great deal of pain." Steve administered oxygen before they put Fred on their gurney.

Red told Anna. "Don't worry ma'am. We'll take good care of him. You're welcome to come with us."

The two muscular paramedics lifted Fred onto a gurney and into their vehicle. They helped Anna into the back of the ambulance so she could ride with her husband while Steve continued to administer care. Red waved to us out the driver's window as they prepared to leave and shot Wendy a quick wink before shouting. "Wendy, we'll call to let you know he's been admitted into the emergency room." With lights and sirens blaring, they left for the emergency room at the county hospital.

Wendy waved back, staring at the ambulance until it was out of sight. We walked up the stairs and onto the front porch. Nate, who heard the sirens, was already waiting there to greet us. Dropping to her knees, Wendy hugged and kissed me. "Max, you are the smartest dog I've ever known. You just may have saved Fred's life with your quick reaction. All part of your amazing training, I'm sure."

Nate asked. "One of the guests told me about what happened to Fred. Did the paramedics say what was wrong with him?"

Wendy shook her head.

"Please keep me posted," Nate said. "I hope he'll be all right. I'll pick Anna up when she's ready to come back, so I'll call the hospital and let them know."

A little more than two hours later, Wendy called Nate to the front desk. "We just heard from Mrs. G. Her husband had a gall bladder attack. She said the symptoms can mimic a heart attack and that the doctors are deciding appropriate treatment for him. He cannot have any more of that fudge ripple ice cream he loves so much and eats every day. His doctors put him on a strict diet until his condition is under control. They advised her that he should see his family physician after they get home. She also said she wanted to thank Max in a big way the next time she sees him. His quick response saved Fred. Now, they'll be able to celebrate their upcoming anniversary."

"I'm glad it wasn't his heart, but even so, gallstones are no fun. I remember how much pain my mother was in." Nate petted the top of my head and smiled. "Max, your amazing reactions and training may have just saved Fred's life. How about you and I make an early day of it? That is, if Wendy has nothing else scheduled for you. We might even be able to squeeze in a couple of magic tricks after dinner."

I was ready for that!

Wendy walked inside with us and took a quick peek at my appointment book. "Nothing more today. Because of Fred's emergency, I cancelled the rest of Max's walks, but he does have an early start for his first photos with the kids as the magician, Max the Magnificent, tomorrow morning at eight thirty."

Nate smiled as he told me, "Okay, Max the Magnificent, let's go upstairs and have a magical dinner before we practice your tricks."

CHAPTER
SIX

The next morning, I woke up bright-eyed and bushy-tailed way before Nate opened his eyes. This was my chance to be his furry alarm clock, so I tiptoed from my bed to outside our bedroom door and took a running leap from the doorway to land right next to him in bed. That 'right next to him' was the tricky part. I have, on occasion, landed on him. Ouch! Today, my aim was good, and I landed next to Nate, but in the process woke him up in a start. I licked his face to calm him down. Once he started to laugh, I knew we were all right.

I couldn't wait to get this wonderful day started. Today's photo day with the kids was my first since I came to The Inn, plus I'd see Aaron later this morning. I hoped I could make him feel even better. This afternoon, I had another walk with Stephanie. I really liked her. Besides, I couldn't wait to see what she bought me at the doggy bakery.

Nate and I had our breakfast before he straightened my Two Turtles Inn bow tie and wrapped me in my Max the Magnificent black cape with red satin around the inside of the collar. We were out on the front steps by 8:30 and saw all the children waiting and cheering with excitement. I couldn't believe my eyes. Every boy and girl who was staying at The Inn must be here.

Some of the girls came prepared with cat ears and whiskers painted on their faces. Tom, our staff photographer, was ready for us. He does weddings, portraits for special events, and now me. It's none of my business, but I think he has a crush on Wendy.

"Max, ready to greet your fans?" Tom asked as the kids squealed with excitement. He faced the children. "Okay, before Max arrived, you all drew numbers. Let's begin. Who has number one?"

A cute little girl dressed in a pink and white striped sundress, wearing black furry cat ears, and sporting painted on whiskers raised her hand. I sat up straight at the bottom of the stairs as she came over and perched on a small chair next to me. I guess she couldn't help herself. I know I'm irresistible. She leaned in…kiss, kiss, kiss, hug. I loved it so much I didn't want her to stop. Tom didn't want her to stop either because he kept shooting. I heard the clicks until he smiled and winked. "Yep, we got a great one." He then called, "Next." Good thing my first walk was at ten. This could take longer than I expected.

After we finished all the photos, Nate waved his arm to get the kids' attention and announced. "Max is performing his first magic show this afternoon at 1:30. You are all invited to the community room to see it. Let's go to the dining room for a very special breakfast."

I followed them inside for more hugs and pets. Oh, how I loved this! Nate removed my cape before he interrupted my lovefest to whisper, "Max, it's ten. Time for your first walk."

I also loved to hear "walk." I jumped up and Nate and I left for the front desk. No surprise. Aaron was already there and greeted us with a huge smile. He had on surfer jams in a fish pattern, an "I'm on Vacation" T-shirt, and carried a tote with a pool towel. His outfit made me burst into a doggy smile. Aaron dropped his tote behind the front desk and said, "Max, spending this time with you makes my day. I can't wait to get started."

Today, my fifth day on the job, I felt in charge and comfortable because I'm loved and love everyone around me. I'm so happy. Because of my service training, I will do whatever I can to help people not just with physical problems but emotional ones. I wagged my tail as Wendy fastened my leash. Aaron and I went down the stairs, over the front lawn, and walked to the short wooded path across from the beach. He passed by the first bench, the second, and stopped at the third one with a view of an Osprey nest. This stop was something new for me, but I liked new things. Aaron took a deep breath.

"Max, yesterday you made me realize there's more to life than work and Beth. Don't get me wrong. I'm still in love with her. My heart still aches. You know I tried to call her again this morning. I know you're thinking 'why bother?', but to my surprise she answered even after checking her caller ID." He ran his fingers through his hair as he continued.

"Because of that, I thought there may be hope for us as a couple, so I began by telling her how much I loved her. What do you think was her immediate response? She asked me never to call her again. 'Please don't', she snapped. 'Aaron, I've made my decision and you're just making it hard on yourself.' Imagine that! I'm making it hard on myself. I love her more than life itself, so I told her that before I begged. 'Beth, please come back to me. I'll change my work schedule. I'll do anything you want me to do. Please marry me.'"

I moved in closer to nuzzle his leg. I sensed how devastated he was. "But Max, since she turned me down again, I decided that would be my last call to her. I can no longer take the pain of her rejection. Pulling myself together, I gathered my pride, and said goodbye. 'Beth, this is my last call. You know how I feel about you because you used to feel that way about me. If this is what you really want, I'll leave you alone. But don't come crying to me when Stu disappoints you.' It didn't take long for her to respond. 'Stu's definitely the man I want. He will not disappoint me. I'm the center of his universe.' I interrupted, 'And you were once the center of mine. It's goodbye then, Beth.' I hung up wondering if our romance would have lasted forever especially after she cheated on me."

Aaron patted his lap, signaling for me to put my front paws up on his leg. Of course, I obliged.

"I've been friends with Stu for a long time and knew he had an eye for the ladies. Beth is beautiful with long red hair and big green eyes. She was Homecoming Queen her senior year in college, but I fell in love with the person. The one who cared for others; the one who loved to read and learn. She's beautiful inside and out. Stu has been in and out of relationships with attractive women his entire adult life. It's like he's with someone until the next shiny object comes along. I hope for Beth's sake, it works, but if it doesn't, what should I do? I'm still in love with her."

He knew I couldn't answer, but I think just getting those feelings out will help him heal.

At that point, Aaron glanced at his watch. "Our time

together flies. Guess we better head back to The Inn." He stood, and we began to walk back.

Aaron talked the entire way. "Like I said, Max, you make me see there's more to life than Beth. I love my work; it fulfills me, so that's a given. After our chats, I decided not to change that just because someone tells me I should. So I guess I need to think long and hard about all of this. Maybe a few more walks with you and I will sort things out."

With that, we reached the front steps of The Inn and went inside to the front desk to see Wendy. Aaron laughed. "You do know you have a certified doggy therapist here, don't you?"

Wendy smiled and took my leash. "I've heard that a few times this week."

Maybe he thought that because I listened, hoping my love and concern will help him make the right decision for his future. Wendy looked at her watch. "Max has one more walk before he'll entertain our youngest guests with a magic show."

Aaron touched the top of my head. "Max, you're a guy of many talents. What time and where? I sure wouldn't want to miss that."

Wendy smiled. "Not sure if you meet the age and height requirements, but it's at 1:30 in our community room. Nate, our innkeeper, will be the master of ceremonies for the show."

Aaron smiled. "I'll walk on my hands and knees if it will help me get in. But maybe I could watch from the hallway."

Wendy laughed. "See you tomorrow, Aaron." Then she whisked me behind the front desk for a quick drink and brushing to get me ready for my next walk at 11:30. Aaron grabbed his tote and left for the pool.

Nate peeked out his office door to see me resting on my bed. He whistled, so I got up and followed him into his office. He said "Sit," before advising me. "Max, I know the kids will love your show, but maybe we should run through your magic tricks one more time to make sure you're one hundred per cent ready."

I knew he wanted everything to be perfect, so we worked through all of my tricks. "Good boy. You'll be great. Now, let's get you back to your concierge station." Nate gave me a couple of small treats to chew and another small bowl of water.

Wendy knocked on Nate's door. "Max has two more walks scheduled for today. I need him out here to finish getting him ready before his next guest arrives."

Nate opened the door to his office, and I walked out to Wendy. At once, she took me behind the front desk and clicked my leash onto my collar to get me ready for my next walk. She held my face in both her hands and looked into my eyes. "You're going to meet Mrs. Betty Brownet at 11:30. I know you'll love her."

CHAPTER
SEVEN

Just when Wendy finished speaking, I heard someone approach the front desk. Mrs. Betty Brownet arrived right on time for her walk wearing a flowered sundress and sporting a small straw hat. Elderly, she ambled toward me at a slow pace like Mrs. Guyer. I wagged my tail and licked her hand to greet her. That made her burst into a smile. She was short, a bit pudgy around the middle, and after taking one look at me, gushed with delight. "Max, you're such a sweetie. I'm sure we're going to get along just fine."

I know everyone loves me because I love them. Wendy handed Betty my leash advising her, "Have fun, you two, but please go slow, and be extra careful walking on the uneven paths. Let Max guide you, since he walks these paths every day."

Betty winked. "I will, dear. Okay, Max, let's get going. I can't wait to get close to that lovely rose garden I can see from my room."

Off we went. I walked so slow I thought I would fall asleep standing up, but that was the only way Betty could keep up with me. I knew where to find that small rose garden. Luckily, it was not too far off the easy walking path. Once there, I could see it was filled with ten beautiful rose bushes, all blooming in different shades and all very fragrant.

I sneezed, which made Betty smile. "Max, you're so darn cute," she said before she bent down to smell each color of rose. "Look at these gorgeous blooms in pink, red, white, yellow, even my favorite mauve."

She breathed a deep sigh. "You know, times like these make me think of my Larry. I've been so lonely since he died and miss him every day. These gorgeous flowers reminded me of how he would stop every day on his way home from work to buy me a rose. He even continued bringing me a rose a day after he retired. We both loved their sweet, soft fragrance. I miss that fragrance, since it reminds me of him and how we met."

She sighed again. "You know, when we were young, we both attended the Chelsea Flower Show in England. That's where we met. He was in London on business. I was sent to photograph the flowers, my first assignment for a major seed company. I stepped back to take a photo of a rose and bumped right into him. When I turned to apologize, our eyes met, and it was love at first sight, like in the movies. I feel his love is still with me and find it difficult to accept the fact that he's been gone four years already."

She stopped and stepped back, to take a long lingering look at the small garden again. A tear rolled down her cheek as she walked to the bench in the center of the garden and sat down. I sat up straight next to her so she could stroke my back. "You know, sometimes I think about finding a companion. No, not another husband. When you've had one as special as mine, he's hard to top. No. Just a male friend; someone to accompany me on walks, someone to share a dinner, maybe a movie, maybe an evening stroll. You get the idea. Don't get me wrong, my women friends are great, but once in a while you do need a man's company." She wiped a tear with her hand. "Thanks for taking me here, Max, and most importantly, thanks for listening."

Her last statement didn't surprise me. I sensed how lonely she was. Each time I saw her in the lobby, she rarely smiled. Not like today with me. I know humans like to talk to me because I listen without judging and show them my love.

Betty stroked my back again and asked. "Where shall we go next?"

I paused to think about her question. A lightbulb lit up in my brain. This time of day, the community room was bustling with guests playing games, having iced tea, lemonade, and fresh-baked cookies. I decided to take Betty back to The Inn and straight to the community room. Betty followed but was surprised by our new destination.

As we entered, she leaned down and whispered in my ear. "Max, what are we doing here with all these other people? I thought you and I would spend time together alone."

These late morning game players always seemed to have fun laughing so loud I could hear them from my day bed when I wasn't walking with a guest. Sure enough, I looked around the room and saw tables with two older gents playing a card game with two older women. Once I spotted a table with only three people, I walked Betty to that table. A well-dressed older gentleman stood and introduced himself. "Hello there, you two. My name is Saul White, and what are yours?"

Saul White smiled from ear to ear. He was tan, appeared to be about Betty's age, and handsome with white hair. He dressed casual in madras golf shorts and an open collared golf shirt.

Betty looked down and pointed to me. "Well, first of all, this handsome young man is Max, The Inn's canine concierge who's available for walks. I'm a guest. My name is Betty Brownet."

By Saul's gaze, I could tell he had an instant affinity to Betty. "Do you play Whist, Betty?"

She shuffled her feet, looking down at them a bit shy. "I do but haven't played in over four years. My late husband and I were partners at our club and condo champs."

"Splendid," Saul responded, walking over to pull back the empty chair. "Would you care to join us? As you can see, we're missing a fourth and Max is welcome to stay here and watch."

Betty pondered his question. So far, so good. She didn't bolt and whisk us out of the room. "I'm flattered by your invitation, but I'm a bit rusty."

"We play for fun. You know, at our age, we have to keep our little gray cells busy. Besides, it's like riding a bike." Saul smiled. "I could sure use help. Playing two hands at the same time is no fun for any of us." Like a proper gentleman, he motioned for Betty to take the empty seat.

"What could it hurt except your score? Guess I'll give it a try." Betty shot him one of her irresistible smiles. "That is, if Max will be all right." I wagged my tail a mile a minute to indicate I was.

"Sure looks like he is," Saul responded, "Please, have a seat. You and I will be a team if that's okay with Ken and Lois Kline?"

The Klines nodded, looking anxious to get back to their

game. I watched Betty. She and Saul hit it off at once. They played, laughed, and appeared happy to be together.

I didn't want to leave them but Wendy, who noticed us enter the card room after our walk, came in to retrieve me when Betty's hour was up. I wanted to stay, especially since I saw the way Saul admired Betty and how happy she was to have his companionship even if for a brief time. Reluctantly, I left with Wendy as their game continued.

Wendy turned to Betty before we left. "Thanks, Betty. Looks like Max had as much fun as you did. I can sense he doesn't want to leave because he keeps trying to pull me back to you, but I need to get him ready for his magic show at 1:30. Just so you know, we'll be closing this room at one to get ready."

"Oh my," Betty puzzled, "how could I forget to bring him back? It felt so comfortable to have him lay at my feet. He is a dear. I hope I can spend time with him again."

Saul picked right up on that. "Say Wendy, I wondered if Max had time open for Betty and me tomorrow."

Wendy smiled. "I know 11:30 is available. Would that work for both of you?"

Saul smiled. "It's good for me, but will that work for you, Betty?"

I looked up to see Betty grin. "That would be fine."

Wendy confirmed the time with them before she took me back to my post. "Max, you are turning out to be quite the matchmaker. Good job. I like each of them and know how lonely they both are. Let's find Nate and get ready for your show."

CHAPTER
EIGHT

After being brushed so many times, I was surprised I had any fur left. Nate took me into his office where I got a better look at my pet dad's outfit. I was amazed Wendy didn't laugh when he walked me to the front desk before my show. He changed from his normal Turtle Inn logo golf shirt and casual pants into oversized khaki shorts with huge pockets, a bright colored T-shirt with turtle suspenders, and an extra-large turtle bow tie. He proceeded to clasp my bow tie for the show, a mini version of his, to my collar. Afterwards we did the red cookie, white cookie trick one more time for practice.

As soon as we finished our last rehearsal, he wrapped me in my silky black magician's cape, which he already told me would double as my Dracula costume for Halloween. He shot me a wink. "Ready?" I wagged my tail, and he led me into the community room.

It looked so different from when I left Betty and Saul. The card tables and chairs were gone, replaced by child sized chairs from our library with Turtle Inn balloons tied to each one. The small chairs faced the front of the room and a small make-shift plywood stage. All the kids from the photo shoot plus a few new ones were seated, chatting, and laughing. As soon as we entered, they giggled, stood, and applauded. We walked onto the stage where Nate motioned for them to sit. Once they did, he began our show's introduction.

"Ladies and Gentlemen, boys and girls, today Max the Magnificent, the most amazing dog magician on Sanibel Island, will perform incredible feats of magic, for a dog that is, right in front of your very eyes. Max, please step forward and take a bow."

I bowed by bending my front paws and lowering my head. Nate continued. "For our first trick, Max will choose between a brown cookie and a white cookie. You do know that dogs cannot tell colors like we do, making this a very difficult trick."

The kids became excited and whispered among themselves. I overheard a few trying to guess the magic behind my trick. Not knowing and trying to figure out how the magic is done makes any magic show fun for both kids and adults. I guessed the oldest among them was ten. To add to their excitement, Nate held up two small square biscuits. "To make this trick even more difficult, I will hide them in my hands." He proceeded to palm them. "Okay, Max, brown cookie."

I sniffed both hands and chose his left hand. He opened it. The kids gasped. I was right. "Good job Max, you chose the brown one."

He gave me the cookie, and I immediately munched it. "To prove this is not a fluke, Max will do it again. We did it one more time when I chose the white one. I then completed the rest of my tricks. I selected a red cookie from a white one, caught a smaller cookie, which Nate dropped from over his head with my mouth wide open and more. The little ones giggled and cheered. I heard someone shout, "Encore, encore," from the doorway. I looked over to see Stephanie who, by the shopping bags she held in her hands, must have just returned from town.

After lining up to pet me, the youngsters enjoyed lemonade and pretzels before they left. Stephanie, who was my next walk, ran in to give me a hug. "Congratulations, Max, you're marvelous."

Nate smiled at her. "He's amazing... really the most popular dog I ever had at The Inn."

Stephanie gushed. "I just love him. Oh, I wanted to get your approval before I give him one of these. I bought them at the doggy bakery in town." She pulled something out of her small bag but held it high enough so I couldn't see what it was. "I hoped to give him one on our walk later."

Nate smiled. "They are fine, but one only each day. He'll get too chubby otherwise."

Too chubby? I'm as lean as a fishing pole. Stephanie gave me another quick hug before she left. She looked so happy, as if all of her stress had vanished. Must have been one amazing shopping trip! I still wondered what else she had in that fancy bag she showed Nate. Guess I'll have to wait until our walk to find out.

CHAPTER
NINE

Energized by my show, I bounced back to the front desk to lap a drink from my concierge bowl as Stephanie stepped out of the elevator carrying that small bag with jumping dolphins printed on it. She was ready for our walk. She'd changed into shorts and a striped T-shirt and walked confidently to the front desk. My eyes followed that mysterious bag all the way.

Wendy smiled and asked. "That's such a pretty blue gift bag. I know I shouldn't ask, but I'm curious. What's inside?"

Stephanie tipped the bag just enough so Wendy could take a peek but kept it high enough so I couldn't. She added. "I already got Nate's approval."

Wendy nodded and handed her my leash. Stephanie gently tapped on my head. "Ready, Max? Let's go."

Like bullets, we shot down the steps, moving much faster than I did with Betty. I loved it. We strode onto the walking path. Stephanie clutched her bag as tight as she could, but something sure smelled great through all the wrappings. We continued to walk down to the last park bench on the trail. Runners passed us as we stopped to sit.

Stephanie dipped her hand into the bag. "Maxie, right now, you're my main man. When I went into town yesterday, I found the doggy bakery I remembered from my last stay here and it was still in business, so I bought you four of these."

She held up a cone shaped cookie stuffed with a cheese filling. "It's a doggy cannoli like the Italian pastry, only it's made from all dog friendly ingredients. My mom is of Italian descent and I loved these as human treats. Still do as a matter of fact, even though my waistline doesn't. I will break one in half. We'll do half before we leave and half when we get ready to return. The other three are in my room for safekeeping."

I sat up and straightened. I couldn't prevent the drool that was falling down my chin. Those treats smelled that good. Stephanie snapped the cannoli in half, and I gently took a piece from her hand. I lay down and ate it ever so slowly, enjoying every crumb. It was the most amazing cookie I ever had. She could have told me I was the worst dog in the world and the taste of that cookie would block all that from my mind. When I finished, I sat up and licked her hand as a thank you.

She hugged me and planted a big smooch on the top of my snout. "Max, you *are* my main man. You appreciate me. That's more than I can say for my ex. Now, where did I leave off on our last walk? Wish you could talk."

I licked her knee, leaving my head there for comfort. "Oh, I remember," she exclaimed. "I told you I worked for a big Tampa marketing firm. We had powerful clients, many of whom were millionaires."

I sure didn't need a millionaire owner. I hit the jackpot

with Nate. His love and care meant more than any amount of money in the world.

Stephanie continued. "I worked on all kinds of marketing campaigns until one day my manager, Morgan, called me into her office. She said she needed a specific marketing agenda for a special client. 'Stephanie, your past performances have always brought us success. Your achievements are immeasurable. All your past and present clients adore you. I have a client who needs that special kind of help to run a political campaign. Tyler Breen, the multi-millionaire horse farmer from Ocala, wants to run for the Senate from Florida. He has never run for office before but has enough cash to make it happen on his own never mind what he's already collected from campaign donors. He needs someone to get his campaign off the ground running. I told him you have those skills.'"

Stephanie sighed. "Max, I was shocked. I never participated in a political campaign. I didn't know what to say except to thank her for her confidence in me. She wouldn't let up. 'Stephanie, I need your answer by five tonight in case I'll need to find another marketing expert. Would it help if you met the candidate?'"

She paused. "I was still befuddled but nodded. Morgan advised me. 'Wait here. I'll try to set up a meeting.'"

Stephanie wiped her eyes, trying to hide tears. I sensed she was stressed, so I licked her knee again. She looked down at me. "Max, believe me, I had no idea what was in store for me. It took about fifteen minutes before Morgan returned to confirm the meeting. 'Tyler is available at two. Please meet us in the conference room. I'll be there as well.'

"I remember looking at my watch, wondering what I was getting myself into. Since it was already one, I went back to my office to work on another client's portfolio. I became so engrossed in my work that two o'clock came all too soon. I raced to our conference room and peeked through the glass wall to see Morgan speaking to a tall, slender man who had his back turned to me. She waved me inside."

Stephanie took out a bottle of water and a small plastic dish. "It's hot today. Let's have a drink." She must have seen my tongue hanging out, so she poured water into the dish for me as she sipped from the bottle before she continued. "As I entered the conference room, the gentleman turned around. He was the most handsome man I'd ever met. No kidding, he could have been a movie star. He was tall, slender, had black coiffed hair with just the right spritz of gray at the temples, and well-tanned, the perfect typecast for a senator. From my guess, he looked about forty-five. When he reached out to shake my hand, his sapphire blue eyes sparkled as they gazed into mine. 'Hi. I'm Tyler Breen, and I hear you know your stuff. Hope you'll consider being on my senatorial campaign team.'

"He was so gorgeous. What woman wouldn't want to be on his team? I remained speechless for a few minutes. By the way Morgan stared at me, I think she got a kick out of my reaction."

Stephanie stopped talking to allow a young couple with a baby carriage to stroll by and continued only after they were safely out of earshot. I understood. She wanted this personal conversation to remain private. "I held out my hand to him," she continued, "And said, 'Nice to meet you, Mr. Breen. I don't know if I can live up to such high expectations.' Morgan interjected, 'Trust me, Tyler, she can.'"

Stephanie sighed. "We sat at the conference table where I questioned him about his life experiences and his stance on specific issues. I knew I couldn't work for him if we didn't agree on most of those viewpoints. The longer we talked, the more I found we had common beliefs, so I agreed to be his campaign manager. Morgan drew up the contract and billing charges while I left the room swooning to use an obsolete term."

Stephanie paused. "We planned to start work on his campaign the next morning, so I needed to set this teenage crush of mine aside. I watched him leave from my office window, turning the head of every woman he passed on his way through the parking lot. I pulled myself together; I had to focus. As soon as I finished reviewing his introductory portfolio, I began to formulate marketing ideas for that handsome Mr. Tyler Breen's Senate race. I researched his opponent online as well as what marketing firm she employed. Marketing is a big field, but the most successful agents are a small group. I cultivated my ideas enough to put an outline together for our next meeting."

I gave Stephanie my complete attention as she looked at her watch. "Oh good, you and I still have half an hour before we need to return, so back to the sad story about my ex. We met the next day, and he liked my suggestions, so I started to put them to work. Tyler, as he wanted me to call him, and I often worked the campaign from different locations, so the only time we could meet was early evening, usually for a working yet relaxing dinner at his horse farm. In the very beginning, we shared meals with a group of staffers to discuss the day's activities, but as we got to know each other better and the campaign moved along, he invited fewer and fewer campaign aids until it became just the two of us. Dinners were more romantic and elegant with candlelight, wine, and butler service and had less emphasis on work. Max, I know you're a dog, but I sure hope you're getting the picture.

Honey, even if you're not, it feels good to get this load off my chest."

I smiled at her, wondering if she thought I could understand. Stephanie moved her hand to stroke my head. "One evening, after we finished our marketing meeting, Tyler invited me to take a stroll around the horse fences in the moonlight. Of course, I said 'yes'. He was so handsome, so elegant. How could any woman refuse?"

She glanced up at the sky. "I remember it was a bright full moon that night, so I should have known I'd go a little crazy. We walked in darkness with the light of that brilliant moon guiding us. All the horses were in their stalls and everyone but his household staff had left. He stopped, placed my hand in his, and looked into my eyes. 'Stephanie, you must know how beautiful you are. Never mind how smart, and I'd like to make our partnership more than just business.' He leaned in and his lips gently touched mine. Of course, I can't lie. I didn't stop him from kissing me again. From that night on, our evenings became filled with more romance than business. We spent more and more time together as I accompanied him on the campaign trail, staying overnight at the ranch when we returned. Our evening walks continued for the first six months of the campaign until one evening, after we came inside from our romantic stroll, he reached into his pants pocket and pulled out a three-carat diamond engagement ring. He dropped to one knee and said, 'Stephanie, you've changed my life for the better. Please marry me. Let's make our relationship everlasting.'"

Stephanie held up her empty ring finger. "I was stunned. Absolutely stunned. I was in love with him so of course I said 'yes.' Our engagement made all the headlines in the state papers even as we continued with his Senate race. I did my best marketing job ever, and he won. The man I loved was about to become a U.S. Senator."

Stephanie sighed. "Our wedding was right out of a dream. Tyler made all my wishes come true. My custom wedding gown of imported Italian satin enhanced with French white lace had a cathedral length train. My bouquet contained all the flowers that grew on the ranch. We said our vows outside on the lawn behind his sprawling estate house. I walked past massive floral arrangements on either side of the aisle as guests in formal attire stood to greet me. A runner sprinkled with pink rose petals ended at a large white wicker trellis garnished with ivy and pink roses. The Governor of Florida, a good friend of Tyler's, married us. Tyler had a rustic barn on the property where he held catered parties so we had the most beautiful wedding reception I ever attended. Tyler idolized me as I did him, so I was sure ours was a match made in heaven fit for life."

Stephanie sighed again. "I had six bridesmaids with Morgan as my maid of honor. The bridesmaids wore lavender crepe gowns, while Morgan looked stunning in a deeper shade of purple. The men wore matching lavender bow ties and pocket squares. The large white tent set up for cocktails and appetizers had champagne fountains and so many different canapes some guests I'm sure thought they were dinner. A country western band played for our reception. All day, I felt like I was in a dream. White gloved attendants served a five -course dinner, and the cake was six layers high decorated with fresh flowers that matched my bouquet."

She petted my head again. "We left that night for a short honeymoon in Bermuda since we had to be in Washington, D.C. four days after our wedding. You know I should have suspected something. Even at our reception, pretty women surrounded him, asking him to dance. Everywhere we went, women were drawn to him, but I really didn't think much of it at the time since he never gave me any reason to question his loyalty."

I nuzzled her knee to soothe her and give her the confidence to continue.

"I left the marketing agency on good terms. We moved to Washington, D.C. after our honeymoon. Because Tyler was a Senator, our social life became a whirlwind of events. We attended state dinners, balls, met movie stars, and sports celebrities. I fell into that lifestyle easily, since many of the socialites and their donor husbands or wives reminded me of past clients. As I always said, some of these folks had 'more money than brains.' The women wore couture clothing, took amazing trips, and lived a lavish lifestyle with maids, butlers, and drivers. My life became more like theirs and less like my old life. I never wanted this time to end. The clothes, the domestic help, the limos desensitized my brain, making me unable to see what was really going on. Like any other Senator, Tyler worked late and had long hours, or so he told me."

Stephanie stopped our talk to say "Hi" to two runners and waited to continue until they ran past by our bench. "He gave me no reason to doubt him until ten months into our marriage, I was preparing his suit for the cleaners, when I discovered a folded restaurant napkin with red lipstick smeared in a kiss and a phone number with 'call me –new number.' I believed it to be a mistake, perhaps a note from an admiring fan or groupie. Maybe a competitor slipped it into his pocket when he walked by, or maybe it was from some woman hoping to meet him. I loved him and wanted to give him the benefit of the doubt. The only way I could know for sure was to call the number. When I called from his office extension at the house, a very sexy voice answered, 'Oh Ty, I can't wait to see you tonight. Glad you received my note. I'll have the champagne on ice and wear your favorite red negligee.' Huh. Funny thing, he told me not to wait up because he said he had committee meetings that would go well into the night.

"I needed to know for my own peace of mind what was really going on and wanted to find out as soon as possible. When Tyler came home later that same night, I pretended to be asleep. Once he fell asleep, I got up and removed his cell from his jacket pocket. I looked at his messages. You know, Max, he had texts not only from that one woman but from ten, and none had anything to do with politics. I later learned they were all willing participants in these romantic trysts. The women ranged from staffers, to lobbyists, to donors, almost what seemed like to me, any woman he met at these functions."

She took another deep breath. "I walked out to our living room and collapsed on the couch, quietly crying my eyes out. He broke my heart. I waited two days until Tyler came home for part of the day to confront him with what I had discovered. He laughed it off, saying, 'All these dates are just part of my job and mean nothing to me, only to our re-election. These women initiated our meetings at donor rallies and are all very well connected and rich. You know how much I love you. They mean nothing to me. You alone mean the world to me.'"

Stephanie pounded her fist on her knee. "That arrogant rat...how could he think that 'our' re-election makes it all right for me to condone his bad behavior. Max, you better believe I was at a divorce lawyer's office the very next morning. How could that egotistical man think I'd believe his cheating was all part of his job? Look at me, Max, do I look stupid?"

I cuddled my head in her hand. I knew how smart she was; after all, she liked me.

Stephanie shook her head. "Anyway, my lawyer advised me I could take him to the cleaners since he was a multi-millionaire with stocks, real estate, and cash, and we never signed a pre-nup. But that's not me. I wanted to be fair despite his deviant behavior. This woman wanted that arrogant man out of my life more than anything. Tyler was generous with the settlement and begged me to stay, but I resisted. We were officially divorced two months ago. I returned to Florida and contacted Morgan about being rein-stated to my former position. She welcomed me with open arms even under such difficult conditions, gave me time to get settled, and take a vacation so as she put it, 'I could catch my breath.' I start work when I finish my visit here. Max, I loved the guy. How could he treat me like that? I respected him, his job, and our marriage. That's why you are the only man I want in my life. Maybe as time goes by, I'll change my mind on that subject, but I'm not ready yet."

My doggy brain couldn't help but think how nice Stephanie was. I wanted to help her. There must be someone maybe at The Inn with whom she could share some fun and would treat her better.

Stephanie glanced at her watch. "Oh, my goodness, we have only ten minutes to get back and I promised you the other half of your cookie for being such a great listener."

She took the other half of the cannoli out of the bag and gave it to me. I devoured it before we walked back to The Inn at a quick pace so we wouldn't be late. We ran up the stairs just in time. Afternoon showers poured down from the sky. The rain came down in buckets, but we happily made it into the lobby without getting wet. Even I don't like wet dog smell. Wendy was relieved to see us as loud thunder roared, and lightning flashed outside the lobby's windows. Stephanie handed Wendy my leash. "Thanks Wendy and Max, see you both tomorrow."

With that, she left for the elevator and waved as she got in.

I really cared about Stephanie. Her story tugged at my heart. I don't speak Human, but I can sit next to someone and after a few minutes pick up character traits from their tone of voice, their hand gestures, and how they react to me. When they speak, I listen and look up at them.

She deserved better than that cheating husband. I wished I could help her, but like I said before I'm a dog and mending a broken heart was not included in my service dog training. She said she never spoke to anyone about this before, I'm sure, meaning other humans. I hope that by getting it off her chest, Stephanie's broken heart will begin to heal.

CHAPTER
TEN

That afternoon, my four-thirty the private portrait shoot on our front steps was cancelled due to bad weather. Wendy decided to take me into the children's playroom to visit the kids. I loved visiting them more than anything. I wagged my tail non-stop as they took turns petting and hugging me. One sweet little girl with braids and ribbons named Crystal asked Wendy if she could take me home after her vacation ended. I'm glad Wendy had to handle that question so I could just lick her face plastered with oatmeal cookie crumbs and snuggle next to her.

My half hour with the kids passed too quickly. I loved to hear their giggles when I retrieved my squeaky toys for them. At four forty-five, Nate came into the playroom to see how the kids and I were doing. He was like a big kid himself and helped the kids toss my toys. I had so much fun I didn't want to leave. Everyone was having such a great time, but playtime was over at five. Nate greeted the parents ready to meet their little sweethearts. On the way back to the front lobby, we spotted Fred and Anna returning from the hospital.

Anna rushed over, knelt next to me and surrounded me with a big hug. She had tears in her eyes as her voice trembled. "Max, how can we ever thank you? Tomorrow, we'll be celebrating our sixtieth anniversary. Because of you, we're both here to celebrate and we'll be able to share more years together."

Nate looked proud as he shook Fred's hand. "Glad to hear you're better, sir. I'm proud of Max for helping you both." He hugged Anna.

One thing I do know is that when Nate's happy, I'm happy. They talked for a while before Nate added, "If there's anything you need, please let me know. I'm always happy to help."

Mrs. Guyer kissed Nate's cheek before we left to start up the staircase to our cozy owner's apartment. Since Nate was single, small, and cozy was perfect for us. Most nights, he was too tired to cook. He worked harder than most people knew because he was in charge of everything that happened at The Inn. With all that responsibility, I'd be beat too.

Tonight, he was too tired to visit our restaurant for take-out, so he heated a turkey TV dinner while I enjoyed my turkey kibbles. Afterward, we crashed on the couch to watch TV. He watches TV. I love to lay next to him on the couch and look up at him. Few guests realize as innkeeper, he's s always on call in case of an emergency but tonight we lucked out...no problems. We fell asleep watching an old movie and went to bed as soon as we woke up.

I slept all night. Nate woke me at 7:30 a.m. so we could have breakfast together. I can't believe how I lucky I was Nate found me. To go from service dog training to nothing would have devastated me since I needed something to do and that something should involve humans. My concierge duties fit me to a T.

Happy to see us, Wendy smiled. I wagged my tail and greeted guests in the lobby while I waited for my first walk. I knew it would be Aaron. Wendy fastened my leash as I diverted my eyes to the elevator doors so I wouldn't miss him. Sure enough, when those doors opened, he was the first one out. He looked happy for a change. Dressed in striped shorts and a Sanibel Island T-shirt, he had a bounce in his step as he made his way to the front desk. "Hey Max, I'm ready to go."

Wendy handed Aaron my leash, and we were off, ready to choose our walking path. He surprised me along the way. "Let's do something different today. Let's head to the fishing pier and see if we can spot any dolphins."

Okay nice suggestion, but there's one thing wrong with that idea. I'm not supposed to go on the pier. I barked as loud as I could and jumped from side to side to try and tell him that. Aaron at last realized something was wrong. He gave me a reassuring pat on the head. "Don't worry buddy. We'll sit on a bench on the grass that faces the entrance to the pier. From there, we can spot any dolphins playing and watch their beautiful fins go up and down in the Back Bay. Maybe one will leap out of the water to say 'Hello'. Max, you should know I would never put you in danger. I only want a quiet place with a different view to sit and talk about what I've learned after spending time with you because of how you've changed my outlook on life."

Sitting and listening sounded a whole lot better to me, so I calmed down. Once we arrived near the pier, Aaron pointed to the water. "It's such a beautiful day. Look how the bay waters sparkle in the sunlight. I see a bench with a wonderful view straight ahead."

A tall woman with long gray hair tied back with a band and carrying a fishing pole spotted us and walked over to introduce herself. "Hello boys, I'm Alicia, The Inn's fishing instructor. Any interest in learning how to catch a fish?"

Aaron shook his head. "No, but thanks for the offer. We're here to observe and connect with nature." She huffed off, appearing disappointed she had no takers. As soon as she left, Aaron led us to "our" bench and sat. He began to speak as soon as I placed my head on his knee.

"Well, Maxie, I learned a lesson last night, one that changed my mind and will more than likely change my life. Like an idiot, I called Beth again, hoping she would give me one more chance. I know you're thinking 'Why?'"

How did he know that question crossed my mind? Aaron continued. "She answered even though her caller ID displayed my number. I could hear Stu commenting in the background. As far as I'm concerned, that backstabber isn't worth my time. Anyway, I begged her once more, 'Beth, please forgive me. I never realized how much my absence hurt you. Please give me one more chance.' Do you know what she told me?"

I could guess. She'd been pretty consistent.

Aaron corroborated my suspicions. "She told me, 'No. You are one pathetic man. Get a life.'"

He pounded his fist on the bench. "Pathetic? Pathetic, because I'm a doctor and care about my patients' well-being or pathetic because I'm successful and tried to give her everything she wanted. Max, that did it for me. I sure would be pathetic if I kept that selfish, uncaring woman in my life. I walked here to the pier to change our viewpoint just like I'm changing mine on life."

Wow...I'm impressed. That was forceful. It would be terrific if he meant it, since he's a great guy. Aaron continued. "Max, I've decided to stop being a mope and start meeting new people. Maybe even date again and it's all because of you."

Aaron held my head in his hands and looked into my eyes. "You listened and helped me realize I needed to restart my life. Thank you, buddy, from the bottom of my heart."

Times like these, I wished I could talk, but all I could do was sit and wag my tail. This was a most welcome surprise. I kept swishing my tail in approval just as two dolphins not too far from the pier put on a show for us, jumping out of the water, flipping fish in their teeth, and swimming close to the seawall to catch more.

Aaron laughed. "They're telling me they like my idea, too."

After their visit, he led us back to The Inn the long way. He had a skip in his step, like someone who just had a big burden lifted from his mind.

We reached the front steps. He was so energized, he exclaimed, "Come on. Race you inside." I was ready and shot up the stairs like a flare. Aaron tried to keep up but was never close enough to come from behind and win. Another Max lesson; don't challenge anyone with four legs when you have only two. Out of breath, Aaron took me inside to see Wendy.

She looked at us. "I guess you two had fun. Thanks Aaron, we'll see you tomorrow."

"You sure will," he responded. "I'll go freshen up for my tennis match later this afternoon. Better behave, Max. I can see you walking a guest from the tennis courts."

Aaron made his two fingers move from his eyes to mine before he turned and left. Wendy was quick to fill my water bowl with fresh water. She gave me a small crunchy biscuit as Aaron headed to the elevator.

"Okay, Maxie, let's get you ready for your walk. You'll be spending more time with Betty Brownet. You know how much she loves you."

Excited, I couldn't wait. Betty stepped out of the elevator, but who was that with her? It was Saul White! Ready for our appointment, they walked over to the front desk with a blue bag like the one Stephanie had the other day.

CHAPTER
ELEVEN

That sweet elderly lady approached the front desk first. Wendy greeted her with a big smile. "Good afternoon, Betty," she said as I sat up and shot her my best doggy grin.

Betty was the grandmother everybody wished they had. I fell in love with her the minute I met her. Looking at her neat hair style, I knew she prided herself on her appearance. She dressed for today's walk like she was meeting her lady friends for lunch. I guessed since Saul was with her, I wouldn't have to wonder if she's seeing him again.

I noticed how slow she walked yesterday, but that would never be a problem for me. I was trained to be helpful to all sorts of folks. Wendy complemented them. "Betty, you look lovely in that pale peach flowered dress and Saul is as dapper as ever in his Hawaiian shirt."

Betty, holding a small blue gift bag, smiled as she fished through the bag's tissue paper to pull out a fuzzy lion squeaky toy. Betty squeaked it once. I popped up and stared at it, wagging my tail like crazy. I loved it and couldn't wait to grab it and squeak it. That squeaking was like a battle cry to play fetch. I was more than ready.

"Wendy, dear, after our card game, Saul and I went to lunch yesterday in the village and found this adorable pet store and bakery. I loved the lion because it matched the color of Max's fur, so I had to buy it for him."

Saul chuckled, adding, "She had so much fun looking, I thought she would buy out the entire store."

Betty ignored Saul's comment and turned to me. "Maxie, do you like it?"

Did I ever! I wagged my tail and tried to gently take it from Betty's hand. Once I did, I squeaked it and licked it good and gooey to make sure she didn't want it back. My job had some great perks until Wendy took my lion away from me.

"You and Nate will have a great time with this in the residence. It's not an outside toy, and I doubt if Betty and Saul want to chase you around the property playing keep away."

They both laughed as Saul responded, "Wish we could."

I let Wendy take my new toy. I can't wait for dinner time tonight. I'll make sure Nate plays with me. Wendy fastened my leash as I licked Betty's hand to thank her.

"Are both of you walking Max?" Wendy asked.

They both nodded. Wendy handed over my reins to Saul. "Well, here he is. Have fun."

Saul, who was more stable on his feet than Betty, held onto my leash while Betty held onto his arm. We went down the side ramp to make it easier for Betty, so I took it slow and steady. When we reached the bottom of the ramp, Saul turned to Betty. "Did you bring your bird guide we purchased yesterday?"

Betty smiled. "I sure did. It's in my pocket, 'Birds of Sanibel Island'."

Saul led us to the Back Bay, almost to the same spot Aaron and I visited earlier. As they sat on a bench close to the water, we all looked out at the beautiful view.

Betty took the guide out of her pocket and opened it just as a large blue gray heron flew onto the seawall to scout for food. "My. He's a beauty. Look Saul, there are some egrets near the pier. There are a group of pink birds flying in our direction. Flamingos? I'd better check my guide." She flashed through the photos of colorful birds. "Why they're called Rosetta Spoonbills, because they have such a lovely color."

"Just like your dress, dear. My late wife Marjorie loved bird watching as well, and I loved watching her, just like I love watching you. She's been gone almost five years and I miss her so. My life changed after her death, sold the big house and my appliance business, moved into a Miami Beach condo, all the while trying to adjust to life alone. Max is a miracle worker to find you and introduce you to me. I love every minute we spend together in our newfound friendship."

Betty interrupted, "I know how you feel. My Larry's been gone four years this week, to be precise. Spending this little time with you has lifted my spirits. I think Max could tell I was down and that's why he brought me into the community room. You're from Miami Beach? I moved to Boca Raton a year ago to be near my son."

Saul's face lit up like a Christmas tree because he liked what he heard. "Why," he laughed, "we're practically neighbors. Close enough so we can see each other after we get home, if you'd like."

Betty smiled and nodded. "I'd love that!"

"Say, I bet if we look around, we'll see all kinds of birds from here on our viewing bench. Look at that small flock of white Ibises eating seeds in the grass?" Saul pointed in their direction. I could smell smoke as Saul appeared deep in thought. "Betty, have you visited Ding Darling National Wildlife Refuge here on Sanibel?"

"You know, all the times I've been here I never have. I know it's a National Wildlife Refuge and always wanted to see it."

Saul slowly put his arm around Betty's shoulder. "Good, we have a date for tomorrow morning. I drove my car here, so I don't have to rent one. We can leave early and have coffee on the way."

Betty smiled. "That sounds delightful."

We sat there for about half an hour before Betty and Saul stood to indicate it was time to go. They were so sweet I hated for my hour with them to end. We walked the circular path back to The Inn and Saul spoke to me. "We're slow about some things, Max, but quick about others. Betty and I would never have met if you didn't escort her into the card room. We knew we liked each other on the first hand and want to thank you."

Betty continued. "We don't know if you can understand what we're saying. I read somewhere that smart dogs like you can understand words on the level of a three-year-old. Anyway, I thought you should start a doggy match-making service at The Inn. There must be a few lonely singles too shy or feel they're not ready to meet someone new."

I wagged my tail. Those words sounded like a good plan, especially since Aaron, for one, came to mind. Be nice if I could get him to stop thinking about Beth. The three of us made it back to Wendy. Betty hugged me. Saul patted my head as he spoke to me and Wendy. "You're a great dog,

Max. Wish I could take you home, but I think you need a younger master like Nate. Wendy, I'm taking Betty to Ding Darling tomorrow morning. We plan to leave early, have breakfast on the road, and return by three. If it's possible, we need to change our morning appointment to three tomorrow afternoon, if that's all right with you."

Wendy nodded. "I don't have Max's appointment book with me. It's at my desk, but I will make a note when I get there and call if there are any changes."

They thanked her as Saul added. "We're going to the Courtside Café for lunch. Another guest remarked how great the food was there." Saul took Betty's hand and escorted her to a waiting golf cart he had booked for their afternoon date.

After they left, Wendy remarked. "They're such a great couple. I hope their friendship lasts. A few more walks to go, but I know you're going to love your last one."

CHAPTER
TWELVE

My next two afternoon walks completed, I knew who would be next and couldn't wait. Stephanie approached the front desk, looking fresh and cheerful.

Wendy smiled. "I can tell by your bag that you've been shopping at Blue's in the village. Retail therapy works for me. I love that store. Blue is my favorite color, and all their items are in different shades of blue. I saw your shorts set in their front window and sky blue looks great on you with your coloring."

Stephanie smiled. "Why thank you, Miss Wendy. And… look at these fab flip-flops with blue sequins to match. They even have an elevated heel." She lifted one foot. "I'm so excited. Haven't been shopping for fun stuff like this in ages. I always had to wear business suits and attire suitable for a senator's wife. No cool stuff like this."

Wendy laughed. "We all need a fun shopping trip. It's a stress buster."

Stephanie agreed. "Big time. Yesterday, I overheard you tell a little girl who was coloring in the community room that your favorite crayon color was blue, so I brought you a little present to thank you for being so gracious to me. Thanks for Max as well." She handed her a small gift bag.

Wendy, taken by complete surprise, opened it to hold up a sparkling necklace. "This is gorgeous! The multiple strands of glass beads are in different shades of blue, from aqua to royal." She gasped. "Thank you so much. I love it, but you didn't have to do this. It's my pleasure to take care of our guests. Best job on the island. Oh, and Fred and Anna appreciated their surprise as well, especially since today's their sixtieth anniversary."

Stephanie nodded. "I'm so glad they liked it and that you like yours. You know, there's a magnetic clasp on your necklace. I love those things easy on...easy off."

Wendy opened the clasp, put the necklace on, and ran her fingers over the glass beads. "Stephanie, it's lovely. Really lovely."

Stephanie looked at me. "Okay, Max, don't worry. I have your treat. Ready?"

I felt so happy I wanted to bark but knew I shouldn't. Once Wendy fastened my leash, Stephanie and I were off down the stairs to the walking path. After walking a bit, Stephanie stopped at the first bench we reached and sat before she pulled half of my cookie from her pocket.

"Here you go. Enjoy, my sweet. Wish I could take you home."

Funny how everybody tells me that, but I know Nate would never let that happen. Besides, I love him as much if not more than he loves me. I gently took the cookie from her hand and lay down by her feet to munch on it. Runners passed us, as did baby carriages and bikes. It was nice to take a break.

As I crunched, Stephanie began. "Max, you won't believe who called my cell last night, Senator Tyler Breen, that arrogant man. Our divorce is final, but I still can't shake him out of my life. Anyway, he told me, 'Stephanie, I know I didn't treat you right, but even with all my flaws, one thing stands out in my mind. You are the only woman in my whole life who stole my heart. I love you. I know I had an odd way of showing it, but I really do miss you. Any chance we can get together for a drink and talk things over?' My jaw hit the floor. I couldn't believe he had the nerve to ask! I can't make up stuff like this."

Stephanie looked up to wave to some kids playing lawn darts before she continued.

"Can you believe that? After all the lies, the hurt, and the pain, he wants to talk things over. Nothing further to talk about as far as I'm concerned, and I told him that right then and there. I never want to go through that heartache again, so I told him he had his chance, but I have a new man in my life. Didn't quite mention my new man was a dog. He went ballistic at that new bit of information, so I hung up."

Wow, hope she didn't put my doggy future in jeopardy. I must have had concern written on my face, because she added. "Don't worry. I didn't mention your name. This morning, a knock on my door woke me up. I grabbed my robe, ran to the door, and peeked through the peephole to see a bellman. I couldn't see his face because he was holding an enormous floral arrangement loaded with irises, lilies, daisies, roses, you name the flower, and it was in there. I opened my door and asked him to bring it inside. He placed it on the coffee table. I gave him a tip and as soon as he left, I looked at the attached note.

'"To my darling Stephanie. Please accept this bouquet as a token of my love. Forgive me and come home. Yours forever, Tyler.' Forever huh? His first forever didn't even last a year. Did that arrogant son of a gun think he could buy me off with some flowers? Not this chick, not with all the bull he put me through. I wanted to send them back to him in the worst way but knew I couldn't, so I called Wendy and asked if anyone staying at The Inn was having a special occasion today. She told me about Fred and Anna. I heard you saved Fred's life. I 've already told you this, but Max, I think you're amazing."

Stephanie sighed. "I met them at breakfast the morning Fred ended up in the hospital. They are such a sweet couple and have the kind of relationship I hope to enjoy someday. As soon as I learned today was their sixtieth wedding anniversary, I swore Wendy to secrecy before asking her to please send a bellman to pick up the flowers and take the arrangement to Fred and Anna's room. I then took a piece of The Inn's stationery and wrote 'Happy 60th Anniversary from an anonymous guest.'"

She took a deep breath and then continued. "Since Wendy had seen the flowers when they arrived, she sounded surprised I would send them to someone else. I knew she was too polite and good at her job to ask. I sent the flowers and note on their way with Gary the Bellman. Before he left my room, I asked him to add a $100 gift certificate to The Inn's restaurant and swore him to secrecy as well. I gave him money for the certificate plus a healthy tip, and he took care of everything. Sixty years deserves something extra special. A short time later, Gary called to tell me that Fred and Anna were elated and surprised."

I gave her my best tail wag. Boy, that Tyler doesn't know what he missed. Stephanie's so generous and thoughtful.

Stephanie mused, "That same morning we met over coffee, Fred told me how he met Anna. Their sweet story could have been a scene right out of a romantic movie."

She looked at me and smiled. "Fred was a graduate student at the time studying archeology at the American University in Cairo, Egypt. One night as he walked through one of the richer Cairo neighborhoods, he saw large carved double doors wide open to one of the mansions. He told me he heard laughter and Middle Eastern music."

Stephanie sighed. "He described the well-dressed people who stood on the porch holding fancy drinks. Some were smoking hookahs. 'It's a party,' Fred told me. 'I had just come out of a late lecture and was dressed in a sports jacket and tie appropriate for a fancy party, so I didn't blink and decided to crash the festivities. I walked through the main part of that beautiful house before going out the back door to a large, manicured garden. There I spotted a young woman sitting alone on one of the stone benches that circled the trunk of a large tree strung with colorful party lights. Her long, dark hair shimmered in the moonlight. I thought she was the most beautiful woman I had ever seen. I attempted to speak to her but since I had been in Cairo but a few weeks, I knew only a few words in Egyptian. She answered me in Egyptian but no matter how hard I tried, including using hand gestures, I couldn't get her to understand me. I was befuddled until she stood and introduced herself in English. Right then and there, when our eyes connected, I knew it was love at first sight. Imagine that?' he mused. 'Love at first sight and today we celebrate sixty years of married life.'"

Stephanie shot me a smile. "How wonderful is that? Looks like you finished your cookie and I'm talking too much. Let's continue our walk."

She didn't know she couldn't talk too much for me. I loved the sound of her sweet, melodic voice. As she stood, she began to wobble not like her at all. She was probably not used to her new fashionable flip-flops. We walked the path and stopped to admire the many beautiful water birds that frequent the island. I knew better than to bark and make them fly off like I do when I'm alone with Nate. But I did turn my head real quick when two cute brown bunnies hopped near our path. I really wanted to chase them, but again knew better. All that training was not wasted on this pup. Anyway, we spotted a couple of humans walking our way.

Stephanie gushed, "Look, Max. It's Fred and Anna." That sweet couple walked arm and arm. Stephanie greeted them. "You two lovebirds look like you're having a great day."

Anna responded, trying to cover tears of joy. "It's our anniversary. Our sixtieth to be exact and some kind guest sent the most amazing flower arrangement I have ever received in my entire life. It was so large and beautiful, and had a note attached with best wishes and a one-hundred-dollar gift card to The Inn's restaurant. We plan on going there tonight to celebrate. I wish I knew who sent it. I'd like to thank that thoughtful person personally. Before we left on our walk, I asked Wendy if that special delivery was from The Inn. She took my hand in that sweet manner of hers and said 'no' but Nate did send us a bottle of champagne and a gorgeous plant. They'll be in our room when we return."

"Everyone makes us feel so special," Fred added.

Stephanie smiled. "You are special to celebrate sixty years of love. I think that's wonderful, especially after Fred's health scare. Your sixtieth is quite a milestone, so you should celebrate in style." Stephanie walked over and hugged them both. I didn't want to feel left out, even though I could only lick their knees.

After our hug, we parted ways. Stephanie and I walked the curved path near the tennis courts. I spotted Aaron, who saw me and signaled back with his fingers that he was watching me. I watched his eyes drift over to Stephanie and linger there for a few minutes. Maybe he heard her noisy flip-flops. From my vantage point, they sure were as loud as they could be. Her heel never missed the back of her shoe at every step. Clip Clop Clip Clop…almost like a horse and buggy.

Stephanie stopped a little further ahead in front of the tennis courts and sat on a bench. She couldn't have noticed Aaron because she paid no attention to the tennis match.

"Max," she told me. "Let's try to make it all the way around the path. Another guest at breakfast this morning said she spotted two flamingos near the docks. If we're lucky, those two unusual visitors will still be there when we arrive."

She knelt over and grabbed at her flip-flops. "These things sure are cute, but not too practical. I'll make it to the docks but will have to walk slower than I like."

I didn't care how long we took. I just loved spending time with her. She stood, wobbled a bit, and walked the path at a speed even Anna and Fred would find slow. When we reached the end of that path, our view of the Back Bay opened up. Stephanie became excited. So much so her voice sounded an octave higher. "Look, those beautiful creatures are still here."

Sure enough, two beautiful flamingos stood tall not too far from us. Boy if I wasn't a trained professional, I would chase them and make them fly. I whimpered, but my whine was interpreted by Stephanie to mean something else. "Max, are you okay? Hurt?'

Then she saw what my eyes focused on and laughed.

"Nate warned me about you chasing birds. Sorry, but you'll have to leave our stately visitors alone. I heard if given the chance, you love to hop with those little brown bunnies that come out of the bushes at dusk. I don't want to encourage you, but I'd love to see that."

Stephanie took out her cell and photographed the two regal coral colored birds. It amazed me they could stand on those skinny legs. She turned and pointed her cell at me. "Sit and smile for me, Max. I've got online friends waiting to meet you. I've e-mailed them and told them all about you! Okay, photo shoot complete, we're off."

Hard not to let her e-mailing photos of me get to my head. I'm ready to meet her friends. Clip-clop, Stephanie wobbled her way around the bend headed back to The Inn. When we reached the tennis courts again, Aaron held up his racket and waved, but she concentrated on her walking so much she didn't notice him.

She walked off the main part of the path a short way to find that small deviation loaded with low clinging vines and small rocks. She wobbled back and forth. I held my breath, waiting for her to regain her footing each time. She giggled. "These flip-flops throw my balance off and make me stagger like I'm drunk."

She took one long step over a few small rocks. I watched as she swayed back and forth and barked, hoping to warn her to get back on the main path, but my bark was not enough to keep her safe. One more sway and down she went. She hit the ground hard and grabbed her ankle. She panicked since there was nothing strong enough nearby for her to hold and help her get up.

She moaned. "Oh, I really did it this time. My ankle's killing me. Never mind how much my leg hurts. I don't think I can get up."

I had to do something. I couldn't leave her there waiting for someone to pass by. I wanted to help her more than anything else, so I tugged at my leash until she let go. I barked and jumped from side to side, trying to tell her I was leaving to get help. Through her tears from pain, she nodded that she understood. "Maxie, go get help." After she said that, a light bulb suddenly went off in my brain. Aaron was a doctor and might still be on the tennis court so I headed there first.

CHAPTER
THIRTEEN

How could I forget for even one second Aaron was a doctor? I shot out onto the walking path, heading straight to the tennis courts to find him. When I arrived, he was talking and laughing with another man, also holding a tennis racket near the net. He wore his usual mismatched outfit, a striped T-shirt and madras shorts. I ran over and interrupted them. I tugged at Aaron's hand.

Puzzled by my actions, he asked. "Max, what are you doing here alone?"

I jumped back and forth and barked as loud as I could.

Aaron studied me a few more minutes. "Is something wrong?"

I jumped once more.

"Why are you still attached to your leash? Is the person you were with in need of help?" Finally, I got through to him. I barked again. Aaron put his racket down and took my leash. "Show me. Max, show me where to go."

I led Aaron down our walking path until we reached the curve where Stephanie lay on her side, holding her ankle.

As we approached, she looked at me with tears in her eyes. "Maxie, thank you. I needed help, and you understood."

Dr. Aaron shot Stephanie a kind smile and in a very reassuring voice responded. "He sure did, Miss. He ran directly to me. Dogs can be a lot smarter than people think. My name is Aaron Swift and I'm a doctor, a vacationing doctor, but still a doctor, nonetheless. Do you mind if I take a look at your ankle?"

Stephanie studied Aaron's gentle demeanor and a weak smile crossed her face before she nodded.

He continued. "Please excuse my attire. I just finished a tennis match when Max came for me. He must really like you. What's your name?"

Stephanie focused on Aaron's kind eyes. "I'm Stephanie Jakes, here for a much-needed break from life. I hope I didn't break anything because Max and I have a standing date every afternoon about this time for a walk."

Aaron flashed an irresistible smile. "He's one lucky guy. Again, mind if I examine your ankle? It may hurt, since I will have to move your ankle and your leg in the process."

"Please do," she replied.

Aaron knelt on the path next to Stephanie and examined her left ankle and lower left leg. "Does it only hurt when you move or is there pain somewhere else?"

Stephanie paused, grimacing. "My ankle and leg pain are excruciating, but I also scraped the back of my leg when I fell. That stings like the dickens."

Aaron moved her leg ever so gently to expose a gash filled with blood and dirt. "We'll need to get that wound treated, so it doesn't become infected."

I watched him press on her left ankle, then on her lower left leg one more time. She whimpered. His exam complete, he returned her leg to its former position. "You'll need x-rays to know whether you have a bad sprain, a fracture, or both. Would you like me to call Wendy and have her send a golf cart to take you back to The Inn? I can take care of Mr. Max."

Stephanie shook her head 'no'. I figured she wouldn't agree to that because she was very independent. Not to mention determined. Since this was Aaron's first encounter with her, he had no idea what he was getting himself into. She answered at once. "I don't want to be a spectacle. Maybe if I could stand, I could limp back on my own steam."

Aaron sounded firm. "From what I examined, that's unlikely. You should avoid putting weight on that leg. You may find it difficult to walk even with a cane or crutches."

"How about human help?" Stephanie asked, looking into Aaron's big eyes.

I could tell her question surprised him. "I'm a doctor and have already advised you. Any weight on your injured ankle can make it and the pain in your leg worse."

Stephanie laughed through the pain. "If you're worried about a malpractice lawsuit, I'll be happy to sign a waiver saying you advised me against walking on it, but I did anyway?"

At that point, I sensed Aaron figured he wasn't going to win because he stood and said, "Okay, let me try to lift you."

I wagged my tail and barked happy when he did.

He struggled before he was able to help her stand. "Guess I'm not as strong as I used to be. Middle age has a way of doing that to you. Delivering babies is not as good a workout as lifting weights. He groaned, trying to keep her standing. "Guess I need more hours in the gym while I'm here. That should also help me look better." He winked.

"You know I try to pay attention to my style, so I do listen to the Fashionistas. I always wear vertical stripes with my plaid shorts to hide my girth."

He pointed to his striped T-shirt and mismatched shorts. His bad joke made Stephanie smile. By their interactions, I saw he enjoyed helping her as she placed both of her arms around his neck.

Stephanie grimaced. "My ankle hurts, but I might be able to walk. I'll put my weight on my good leg."

Aaron shook his head. "Not so fast. Look at your lower leg. It's turning colors. Bruising may indicate it may be more than a sprain. Anyone ever advise you to wear more sensible shoes? Those flip-flops may be good around the pool, but that's all."

Stephanie groaned. "I know, but I just bought them today and couldn't wait to wear them. The very last thing I need to hear is a know-it-all lecture."

Aaron shrugged. "That's a not very nice thing to say to someone who's trying to help you. Maybe I should put you down and leave you here." He started lowering Stephanie, but still held her in his arms. I barked at her, hoping to woof some sense into her bad attitude.

Stephanie became quiet. I think she sensed we'd both tired of her attitude. She responded in a quiet voice. "You're right. I apologize for being rude. I don't know what came over me. I do appreciate your help more than you can imagine. I never should have worn these flip-flops on the walking path, but they were so cute. I always wear proper walking shoes to walk Max."

Aaron sighed as he juggled her in his arms. Her weight must be getting to him, but even so, I think he liked her being so close. He nodded. "Apology accepted. Let's get going, so we can get that gash taken care of."

He tried to readjust her position. "I knew I never should have stopped strength training. Come on, Max. Follow us. I can't hold your leash and Stephanie, too."

I tracked behind them as we headed back to The Inn. Aaron stopped every so often to adjust Stephanie's weight. We passed two walkers we didn't know. The woman smiled after she saw us and said, "Oh, honey, how sweet is that? They must be honeymooners. Remember when we did things like that?"

Her husband responded. "Yes, dear, but you were a bit lighter then. Look at that cute dog. He follows them without a leash. Wish our Oscar would do that."

I shook my collar because I'll bet Oscar didn't have service dog training. As soon as we passed the tennis courts, I knew we didn't have far to go.

Aaron, a bit out of breath asked, "Stephanie, are you feeling all right? I'm trying to get you there as quick as possible. I have a small medical bag in my room safe. I'll put you down on the lobby couch and have Wendy call for an ambulance while I go get it so I can clean your wound while we wait."

Stephanie studied Aaron's eyes, paying no attention to his mismatched tennis outfit. "Your eyes tell me you're a compassionate and caring person. Definitely not the type of man I've been used to. Thank you for all the help."

Aaron looked puzzled by that remark. The Inn was now in our sight so I broke away from them and raced to find Wendy. She was eating lunch behind the front desk. I barked my most stressful bark. Surprised to see me without a guest, she put her tuna sandwich—my fave to find on the floor—down on her plate and ran over to me. "Max, what happened? Last time you came back like this, Fred was sick."

I barked again. She didn't hesitate. "Let's go. Show me where to go."

We raced past the front desk as she grabbed the portable desk phone to take outside. From the porch, we saw Aaron hobbling along with Stephanie in his arms. Wendy ran down the steps dialing the paramedics on the way. Aaron made it to The Inn's front steps where, with Wendy's help, he assisted Stephanie into the nearest lawn chair.

"She fell on her walk with Max. She wore those flimsy flip-flop shoes and crashed, falling into the pebbles and dirt. She has a huge gash on the back of her leg and, at the very least, a bad sprain or fracture that may require x-rays and an MRI. I'm going to my room to get my medical bag."

Aaron dashed up the front stairs and into the elevator. He returned shortly wearing a solid color golf shirt and carrying his leather bag with A.S.M.D engraved on it. "How are you doing, Stephanie? I have what I need to treat your wound, but it may sting."

He opened his bag and took out some supplies. He gently turned Stephanie's leg sideways. I sat by her side the entire time. She petted the top of my head for comfort, saying. "Max, you're my main man."

I smiled a doggy smile and panted, happy she was going to be all right. Aaron cleaned the wound before treating it with antibiotic cream and a big bandage. He finished just as the paramedics pulled up. Wendy waved them over. "Red, we're over here!"

Red, the lead EMT who Wendy said was nicknamed because of his bright red hair, climbed down from the driver's seat and greeted her. "Hey, how's my girl? Take it easy on your guests. You've been sending us a lot of business this week." He chuckled before instructing his partner.

"Okay, Steve, get out the gurney. She may not be able to walk on her own."

Steve removed the stretcher from the back of the vehicle.

Aaron interrupted them. "Excuse me, I'm Doctor Swift. Ms. Jakes, my patient, has a definite ankle sprain with a possible fracture to that ankle and her lower left leg. She will need x-rays and an MRI. I just finished treating her wound."

Red, wanting more information, asked, "Excuse me sir, are you the new on-call doctor for The Inn?"

"No, I'm just a guest, but I am a doctor from Boca Raton. Max came to get me after she fell. I would like to accompany her to the hospital. I'm sure you understand how concerned we doctors can be."

"Fine, but you can't ride in the ambulance. You'll have to drive your own car."

"No problem. I planned on doing that since Stephanie will need a ride back to The Inn."

Aaron left, racing around to the back parking lot for his car. It took mere minutes before I saw him driving his fancy convertible sports car with…what's that? Is that a cat on the hood? I glanced over at Wendy, who looked impressed. I'm disappointed in her since for as long as I've known her, she's always told me she was a dog person. "Wow, Max, a silver Jag. That's quite impressive. Old Doc Aaron must do well for himself."

Stephanie stopped moaning when, by the surprised look on her face, she noticed his cat car as well.

Steve returned with the stretcher and the two EMTs prepped Stephanie for her transfer to the hospital. They moved the gurney next to the lounge chair and together slid her onto it. Wendy and I watched. I remembered how great they were with Fred.

Wish I could go too, but since I'm no longer a service dog, I wouldn't be allowed in the hospital. Stephanie winced when they transferred her into the ambulance. I'm sure her twisted leg still hurt. She waved and shouted., "Wait for me, Maxie. Promise I'll be back ASAP."

The ambulance left with no lights or sirens, unlike the time they left with Fred because Stephanie's condition was not a medical emergency. I watched Aaron's cat car follow them. I looked up at Wendy as she touched my head.

"Max, you are the best dog I've ever known and our hero once again," Wendy said. "How about a treat? Stephanie's in good hands and I'm sure she'll be back here as soon as she gets x-rays, finds out what's wrong, and receives appropriate treatment."

I followed Wendy up the front steps to my basket bed. I was way too tired for the peanut butter cookie Wendy placed under my nose. This life-saving business was exhausting. Collapsing on my bed, the smell of that cookie didn't distract me from snuggling into my soft pillow, knowing that once in a while sleep was better than cookies.

CHAPTER
FOURTEEN

One sniff of the cookie Wendy left earlier, along with happy chatter, woke me from my delightful dream about catching our neighbor's pesky cat that sneaks onto our property at dusk to hunt for mice. Even though the cookie aroma reached my brain, my mind was still not awake enough to decipher who was speaking. It took a few seconds before I recognized Aaron's voice and Stephanie's laugh as well as Wendy asking questions. I ate my cookie, stood, and stretched my back legs before greeting everyone.

"Well, look what the sandman brought us. Sleepy Max is awake." Aaron laughed.

Stephanie seated in a wheelchair responded, "Poor baby. He exhausted himself rescuing me. Maxie, as I told you a thousand times before. You're the best."

Wendy looked at me with her irresistible gaze and agreed. "He sure is. We're lucky to have him. So, Stephanie, tell me more about your emergency room visit."

Stephanie smiled, "First of all, I've never seen a more handsome bunch of paramedics in my life. They should make a calendar and sell it for charity. Not only were they easy on the eyes, but kind and caring. Someone could write a romance novel and make any one of them the hero. Anyway, when we arrived at the hospital, they wheeled me into admissions, then into an exam room to wait for the doctor. He ordered x-rays. They discovered I have a fracture in my tibia, the lower part of my leg, and a bad ankle sprain. Aaron was so wonderful. He waited patiently for me the entire time."

Aaron interrupted. "I spoke with her attending physician before we left to come back to The Inn, and he said the MRI revealed she had a clean hairline fracture. She's stable, so no surgery needed. She has to keep her fractured leg elevated as much as possible, keep her sprained ankle wrapped, and walk with a cane only when necessary. I know this wheelchair looks like overkill, but she can elevate her leg this way while keeping her weight off of it. She did have a grueling morning. Thanks for having the staff take it out to my car."

Wendy cheered. "That good news calls for a celebration. Would either of you like some iced tea or lemonade? I just made both and they are waiting for you in the community room. By the way, Stephanie, the paramedics make a calendar every year and Red and Steve are in it. I'll e-mail you when next year's becomes available."

Stephanie laughed. "I'll be the first in line to buy one. Now, lemonade sounds great. Thank you. I guess I'll have to cancel my upcoming walks with my little buddy. I'm sorry to have to do that. It was always the brightest spot of my day."

I was really bummed out as well, since I just loved Stephanie. I looked at Aaron. I could see by the look in his eyes that a light bulb just flashed in his head.

"Hold on, Stephanie, if Wendy can arrange for you to

use the wheelchair during your walk times with Max, I'd be more than happy to wheel you and Max could walk next to the chair."

Wendy liked that idea. So did I! She added, "Yes, providing there are no more emergencies that would take precedence for this chair."

I could tell how happy they were with that arrangement because both their faces beamed. Stephanie interjected, "You all are too good to me. See you tomorrow afternoon, Max. Aaron and I are off for some of those homemade cookies and lemonade in the community room before I go up to my room to elevate my leg."

I watched Aaron help Stephanie stand from the wheelchair and hand her a cane. He placed his arm around her back for added stability as they walked into the community room. They both looked so happy. I hope they stay that way and will try my best to make that happen. I yawned a loud yawn. Nate must have heard me because he popped out from his office. "Hi, Wendy. How's Stephanie doing? She had quite a day, but our Max is a hero once again."

Wendy shot Nate a smile. "He sure is and tired himself so much he had to take a nap." Nate returned her smile before glancing down at me. Sometimes I think I can sense some chemistry between them, probably wishful thinking. Nate spoke to me. "Look at the time. It's almost dinner time. Let's go, Max."

Thank goodness. That doggy cookie was great but didn't cut it for a growing lad like me. Nate and I went upstairs to have dinner, snuggle on the couch, watch TV, and carve some Z's.

———

Bright morning sunshine streamed through our bedroom windows. I woke up, rolled over, and kicked my paws in the air. I couldn't wait to start my day because it was my first meeting with Carl, our county animal officer. Yesterday morning, Wendy told me. "Carl comes by monthly to instruct our kids on all things dog. He starts early with an 8:30 a.m. presentation. Tomorrow he'll demonstrate the proper way to approach an unfamiliar dog, and, through photos, introduce the kids to our county shelter and the fabulous animals that can be adopted there."

She continued. "You're going to love serving as his demonstration dog because after his presentation, all the kids will all want to line up and pet you."

Wow. I'll have to exhibit my best self-control because I'll want to kiss each and every one of their adorable little faces!

Carl's presentation was so exhilarating I wanted to be his demonstration dog all over again. The kids paid strict attention to his talk and asked good questions. As soon as he finished, the kids lined up, just like Wendy said, to pet me. How wonderful! Afterward, they enjoyed a full country breakfast of bacon and scrambled eggs. While they were munching, Officer Carl pulled out a big dog biscuit from his pants pocket and gave it to me. Hope he cleared it with Nate, because once it was in my grasp it was too late.

Officer Carl explained to the kids why they shouldn't take food from the mouth of a dog who's eating, so I enjoyed my cookie in peace. When we finished, Carl took me back to Wendy, who noticed some large crumbs on my chin and, in her motherly fashion, wiped my face with a napkin. "Max, you know The Inn can't have a messy concierge. You must always look your best."

I knew but that oversized cookie made oversized

crumbs. She squeezed and kissed my face before thanking Carl. "On behalf of The Inn, Nate wanted me to thank you, Carl, for your monthly visits with our kids. He asked me to present you with this gift certificate for two complete dinners and a bottle of wine in The Sanibel Vista, our Inn's restaurant, for you and your wife to enjoy."

Wendy handed Carl an envelope with turtles on it. He smiled. "My Stacy's going to love this. Thank you. It's our fifth anniversary next week, so tell Nate he has great timing. What a great way to celebrate, and Stacy can meet Max. I'll tell her all about you, buddy, and we'll call ahead for a reservation for dinner and Max." With that, Carl petted my head and left. Nice guy.

I dashed over to my water dish for a quick drink just as I heard the elevator doors open. I turned to see Aaron wearing his usual mismatched tennis clothes. He really needs a woman's touch. Bet Stephanie could help with that.

"Hi Wendy. Max all set? I'm psyched about our walk today. Don't forget, I booked two hours with Stephanie this afternoon and hope to use the wheelchair."

Wendy fastened my leash and handed it to Aaron. "You're all set for both."

Aaron and I left The Inn and walked our regular path, stopping to look at some beautiful tri-color herons near the water's edge. After about fifteen minutes, Aaron found a bench and we stopped to "chat" as he liked to call it.

He stroked my back. "Hey Max, thanks for yesterday. I'm sorry Stephanie hurt herself, but if you didn't come for me, we never would have met. I don't know what she thinks of me. She was very chatty and friendly during the community room's refreshment hour. She's definitely someone I'd like to know better. By the way you watched out for her, I surmise you really care about her. I think you're a good judge of character."

I know I am, so I continued to listen.

"Besides being attractive, she's funny, and smart. I don't know anything about her past, especially her love life, but maybe will after our walk later today. I'll ask her if I could take her to the Courtside Cafe for a drink or a fancy coffee and hope I'll be able to delve into that. Of course, I'll tell her about my split from Beth."

I licked his knee to show my approval.

"I hope she'd like to go to dinner with me tomorrow night, but I want to be upfront about my being a workaholic before we embark on any kind of date. For some reason, I don't think that will bother her as much as Beth since Stephanie mentioned how much she loved her marketing job at afternoon refreshments."

We sat silent for a long time. Not like his usual chatterbox self. I don't have to wonder who he was thinking about. Aaron stroked my back as we watched some of the beautiful birds that visit our island. All of a sudden, he glanced at his watch. "Wow. Max, our hour's almost up. We're going to have to run to get back on time."

He stood, and our race against time began. Despite the frantic run, we reached Wendy only a few minutes late. No time for a cookie, just a quick water break. I slurped my water so fast, some dripped on the lobby floor in front of the welcome desk. Wendy cleaned it up.

I turned, surprised to see the Forrest Twins. Thank goodness Mrs. Forrest was with them. "We're here for our walk with Max. I'll take his leash. The boys will follow." Wendy reluctantly handed my leash to her. Mrs. Forrest sensed that, adding, "Don't worry. The twins will behave. I promised them pizza for lunch if they did."

Her bribery worked like a charm. We had a peaceful walk and returned at noon. They left for pizza. I hit my water dish and enjoyed a cookie. Wendy petted my head. "You're such a patient dog, especially with those two boys. You'll be happy to know your next walk isn't until two."

Finally, some "Me" time. I enjoyed my rest and greeted a few new guests while I waited for my two o'clock. Betty Brownet and Saul walked arm in arm to the front desk. Excited, I shot up to greet them. Saul chuckled, "Take it easy, Max. We can wait for you. You're definitely worth the wait. Wendy called us just as we returned from Ding Darling and asked if we could move our appointment time up to accommodate another guest, Stephanie Jakes, who injured herself. We met Stephanie at one of the afternoon refreshment hours. She's so sweet and friendly, we're sorry to hear about her injury. Since we had already returned, of course we said 'yes'."

Betty spoke to Wendy. "We had such a lovely day at the park. There was so much to see and photograph. Beautiful birds, tropical plants, scenic ponds, and even a large resident alligator. We left early this morning and stopped for breakfast at a cute cafe on the way. You know, dear, Saul and I owe this furry little guy our happiness since he's the reason we met. Max, keep up the good work and help other lonely souls."

Trust me, I would love to match the entire single world, but it's much tougher than it looks. Once I finished a quick drink, we left for our walk. I saw how enthralled Betty was by all the beautiful birds. My eyes bounced back and forth between her and Saul, staring at her. We stopped at the nearest bench for a break as Betty began to talk to me.

"I found out that since Saul and I don't live too far from each other, we made plans to see each other after we get home. We met late in our stay, and both have to go home tomorrow. I called my son to tell him not to come get me. Saul is giving me a lift home. Of course, my son Ted was concerned because I was travelling with a man I didn't know very long, but I assured him I'll be just fine."

I hope they'll both be fine. I find it funny that humans talk to me like I understand. Wonder if they realize that dogs can understand some words, but it's their tone of voice that makes them listen. Anyway, I'm glad they'll get together after they leave The Inn. They're both so nice.

We took our time walking back. Betty mused. "Oh, I've had such a wonderful time. I hate to leave this lovely scenery, the beautiful birds, but most of all Max."

Saul responded, "I have a strong feeling this Inn hasn't seen the last of us." When we reached the front desk, he handed Wendy an envelope. "We're leaving tomorrow morning and we wanted to get our buddy Max a thank you gift for introducing us. It's a gift certificate to the doggy bakery. This way, Nate can pace his treats and this other gift certificate is for you, Wendy, to find something special at Sanibel Gifts."

Wendy looked surprised to say the least, but as I always believed, if you're nice to people, they're nice back. Saul petted my head. "Max, this is our last day here. We hate to leave you but hope to return soon perhaps for a long week-end. We want to thank you for introducing Betty and me."

Betty knelt, gave me a hug, and kissed the top of my head. I adored it. Saul followed her lead a bit teary eyed and shook my paw. "Great dog you have here, Wendy. Take good care of him."

Wendy smiled. "Max gets the best care."

Saul turned to Betty. "How about that late lunch I promised you?"

Betty smiled. "Well, what are we waiting for?"

They walked arm in arm into The Inn's coffee shop for their late lunch as I took my position next to the front desk to greet new check-ins. A few minutes later, I heard the elevator doors open. I saw Aaron help Stephanie walk with her cane to the front desk. Wendy hurried into the back room to get the wheelchair. Aaron and Stephanie were all smiles.

Stephanie gushed, "Oh Maxie, I'm so happy. I thought I wouldn't be able to walk you again. But Aaron is making this possible. How wonderful is that?"

Stephanie winked before reaching for something in her pocket. "And I didn't even forget your cookie."

Wendy returned with the wheelchair. Aaron, the perfect gentleman, helped Stephanie get comfortable in the chair before he took my leash. Busy day, I needed that brief time off. We walked the path facing the Back Bay. Aaron beamed, appearing much happier than usual. Even his tone of voice sounded more cheerful. We stopped for a break at our favorite bench. Aaron assisted Stephanie out of the wheelchair. Once seated, Stephanie pulled out that doggy cannoli from her pocket and gave me half. I ate it ever so slowly. It was that good.

"Good boy. I'll give you the other half before we hit The Inn." Stephanie stroked my fur. I just loved her to pieces!

Aaron watched us and smiled the kind of smile you have when you're with someone special. He cleared his throat, interrupting our love fest. "So, Stephanie, have you been to this Inn before?"

She nodded. "As a matter of fact, I have. My ex was running for Senate from Florida. It was an exhausting campaign, and we needed a brief respite. He did a rally in Ft. Myers not too far from here, so we played hooky for two days and came here for a break. We hoped to return for a longer stay, but since we're not together anymore, that didn't happen. It's such a lovely location on the Bay with a Gulf front beach just across the road, plus all the beautiful wildlife on the property, not to mention the incredible staff. But, of course, they didn't have Maxie back then. He makes it extra special. Have you stayed here before?"

"I have as well. We…I mean, I really loved the place. Beth and I hoped to come back after we were married. Like you, that didn't work out. It's a long story I'll save for some other time. Today we should enjoy ourselves and watch the dolphins play."

"Ditto to that," Stephanie chimed in smiling.

I barked at one dolphin when he swam close to the seawall. He was beautiful, and I had overheard from a couple of Nate's buddies that dolphins love dogs and can hear us bark, so I kept barking even though I knew it was against both my service dog and concierge training. The dolphin swam in as close to us as he could and flipped his tail. As he swam away, he jumped out of the water with a fish he caught in his mouth. Aaron and Stephanie observed him in wonder. I settled down and stopped barking. Sure hope they don't tell Nate about my bad behavior.

"Max," Stephanie blurted, "That dolphin was as incredible as one I saw in an aquarium show. Your bark brought him in to see us. We'll have to dub you the dolphin whisperer."

Nice, but still hope she doesn't tell Nate. They sat a bit longer before Aaron told Stephanie about his plans for the afternoon. "You know, I asked Wendy for two hours with Max if he wasn't all tied up." He laughed. "Bad joke. She gave me the okay, so I wondered if you'd like to go to the tennis center. They have a really nice refreshment center.

Thought we could get a cold drink and watch the tennis players practice."

Stephanie's face lit up like holiday lights. "I'd love that. I never visited the tennis center, but just being outside with you and Max is wonderful. I appreciate you letting me tag along."

Aaron smiled, proud he had such a great idea as Stephanie added, "Whether we go anywhere or not, being with the two of you always brightens my day."

Aaron helped Stephanie up from the bench and into her wheelchair. No one held onto my leash, but I really didn't want to be anywhere else. I was having too much fun and wanted to stay with them. Once ready, he pushed Stephanie's wheelchair back onto the path and we left for refreshments. Water and doggy treats sounded pretty good to me but hearing him ask Stephanie out for a real date would be an even better treat.

CHAPTER
FIFTEEN

I couldn't wait to visit the Courtside Café. Nate never took me there. He was too busy during the day and too tired after work. We were late for lunch and early for dinner, but even so, as soon as we arrived, I saw loads of guests enjoying refreshments while watching the tennis players. Wonder if they all were waiting for me? The cafe had indoor seating, and an outside screened patio facing the courts. The players wore fancy coordinated tennis clothes, unlike Aaron's current fashion statement of a striped golf shirt and plaid shorts. I repeat. He could really use a woman's touch.

Aaron had us wait at the patio entrance to be seated by the hostess. A cheery server with long brown hair tied back with a ribbon and wearing a uniform greeted us. "Hi Aaron, I missed seeing you on the courts today. Do you need a table for two?"

Aaron chuckled. "Thanks, but that's three, Rachel." as he pointed to me.

She took one look at me and couldn't help herself. "Hi,

sweetie. He's so cute and fuzzy. Is he our famous canine concierge, Max?"

I smiled and wagged my tail.

"He sure is." Aaron appeared impressed with my fame.

Rachel patted my head. "Well, this calls for a special table on the patio, of course. Please follow me."

She took us to a courtside table with a great view of the tennis practice. First, we walked by patrons enjoying fancy tropical drinks with mini umbrellas and great smelling appetizers. As my nose went wild, Rachel took a chair away so Aaron could help Stephanie roll her wheelchair up to the table and place her cane against the wall behind us. Once we all were comfy, Rachel brought out a big bowl of water for me along with two glasses of iced water and some menus for my humans.

My nose turned to take in all the wonderful aromas coming out of the kitchen. My stomach rumbled for some, but as Nate always reminded me. "No people food…not healthy for a dog."

Stephanie smiled. "Aaron, thanks for bringing me here. It makes me feel normal, like I can get out into the world and experience new things even with my injuries."

Aaron watched Stephanie study the menu. By his dreamy gaze, I could tell he was really into her. "I have a suggestion," Aaron began. "Why don't we have an appetizer and one of those fancy cocktails and come back later for dinner? It's beautiful here at night. They light the hanging lanterns that surround the patio. I don't feel comfortable eating alone in the formal dining room, so I come here for dinner every night. This café has become my hang-out. Since it has outside seating, maybe we can talk Nate into borrowing Max for our dinner."

I heard my name and wagged my tail. I do that every

time someone says, "Max." Besides, I'd love to come back here tonight with Stephanie. Aaron sure didn't waste any time asking for that date, and Stephanie accepted his invitation right away. "That sounds wonderful. I'm looking forward to dinner with you and, hopefully, Max. I usually eat in the dining room alone. The casual atmosphere here is more fun, plus I'll be with my two favorite guys."

She studied the menu. "Any suggestions for an appetizer? What's your favorite?"

Aaron laughed. "You know I'm a doctor, so I try to eat healthy every chance I get, but for some reason, I feel like the steak fries. They bring out a cheese sauce that clogs your arteries and ketchup that raises your blood sugar. Want to live dangerously? Maybe a large basket of steak fries and two Pina Coladas?"

"You sure know how to live dangerously. Sounds good to me too. I haven't had a Pina Colada for what seems like forever."

It was hot out here, so I delved into my water bowl. I picked my head up and wagged my tail at the thought of coming back for dinner. As for now, I've never had French fries before. Maybe one will drop on the patio floor and once it hits, and I'm fast enough, it's mine. Just as I was daydreaming about those fries, Rachel came back, and Aaron gave her our order, reminding her about the cheese sauce and ketchup. I watched as two players came off the court nearest us and greeted Aaron. "Hey guy, we missed you this morning. Who's this lovely lady?"

They looked at Stephanie as Aaron introduced them. "Mark and Cindy, this is Stephanie Jakes, and have you met Max, The Inn's canine concierge?"

Mark, one of Aaron's tennis friends, answered, "Stephanie, very nice to meet you. Watch out for this guy.

He's a formidable opponent. I haven't been able to beat him yet in singles play. Max, it's an honor. For a young dog, you're already a legend here. Sorry we've got to run, but we have to dress for an early dinner reservation." Before they left, they each petted my head.

Rachel returned with their drinks in tall glasses with mini umbrellas and their food order, along with the sauces, two small plates for sharing, and napkins.

"Wow, those fries do look delicious," Stephanie gushed.

"Help yourself," Aaron responded as she used her fork to put some on her plate. He followed suit after placing some cheesy sauce and ketchup on her plate for dipping. All I could think was "Drop one...I dare you just one" as they began to eat.

She took a bite and giggled. "This so reminds me of my high school days a million years ago. I would go out with my friends to an ice cream parlor, and we'd order a plate of fries to split. For some reason, sharing that plate of fries made whatever difficult conversation we needed to share easy. Maybe that's because fries are not formal or fancy."

"Happy times I hope," Aaron added.

"They sure were," Stephanie took another small helping. "Oops. How could I be that clumsy?"

As if in slow motion, I watched that French fry slowly leave the corner of the table and float down into my mouth. I tried to chew it right away, but it was way too hot. I spit it out to cool it by licking it before eating it as quick as I could since Aaron looked like he was ready to grab it. It even had a little bit of sweet stuff on it that made it taste even better.

Aaron couldn't help himself and laughed as he watched me devour it. "Max, you're getting away with murder."

Stephanie giggled before saying, "We can't tell Nate about this. He might not trust us with Max again."

My French fry catching may have contributed to Aaron and Stephanie's new relaxed attitude and helped them open up to each other. I guess what Stephanie said about those French fries was true. Those delicious sticks of potato sure made them talk.

Aaron began. "When Beth broke our engagement, I didn't think love would be part of my future. She was my entire world. Since I'd already paid The Inn for our honeymoon and it was too late to get a refund, I decided to use the reservation. I'm glad I did. I'm having so much fun spending time with you and Max and making new tennis friends. Between my work and my cancelled wedding, I was burned out. When I first arrived, I didn't care if I ever talked to another person again."

Stephanie munched on a fry. "Me too. My divorce and dealing with my no-good ex drained me. I needed an emotional break since as soon as this vacation ends, I go back to work. I've met some wonderful people here, including a dog named Max, and a doctor named Aaron, and plan to enjoy the rest of my time even with my injuries."

I loved her attitude. I sat up, placed my head on her lap, and stared into her eyes.

She petted me but tried to read my mind. "No more fries, Max. Sorry. I don't want to make you sick. You're much too precious. How about the other half of your cookie?"

I can live with that, but right now I wasn't interested in food, only Stephanie's attention. She gave me my cookie just as Rachel stopped by. "Can I get either of you anything else?"

Aaron paused. "Yes. Is there any chance of making a

dinner reservation tonight for the three of us at say seven thirty?"

Rachel's wide eyes twinkled as she looked at me. "Max, you've got them eating out of your paw. Aaron, I'll check on that right away and if confirmed, come back with your reservation card."

Stephanie smiled, pleased at her dinner prospect. "Aaron, I'd love to join you and Max for dinner, but I hope you're not doing this because you feel sorry for me. I can always get room service or ask one of the staff to push me into the main restaurant. I appreciate what you're doing more than you can imagine and would love to come back and share a casual dinner. I took a peek at the menu before we ordered the fries. The choices here are amazing."

Rachel returned in a few minutes and handed Aaron his reservation card. "You're all set for seven thirty and I'll be your server. I happen to be working a double today.

Aaron shot her a smile. "Thanks, Rachel. I'm glad we'll be in your section. You've always taken the best care of me. Well, now that our French fries have been devoured and our drink glasses emptied, it's time to head back and ask Nate about Max."

Aaron charged the bill to his room as Rachel gave Stephanie her cane to hold. Aaron pushed her wheelchair away from the table. All the way back, I kept hoping Nate would say "yes."

CHAPTER
SIXTEEN

W hen we arrived, Wendy was busy checking in two new guests. They both fired questions at her about rates and amenities. When she spotted us, she interrupted their questions to introduce me. "Mr. and Mrs. Brench, I'd like you to meet Max, our canine concierge. He's not only our greeter, but he's available for walks or just to sit with and spend some quiet time. I have his appointment calendar here at the front desk, so contact me if you'd like to make one."

Mr. Brench, who must have been a basketball player because he looked ten feet tall, leaned way down and petted the top of my head. His attitude changed almost at once. "Max," he said, "I'm impressed. I've never met a dog with his own appointment schedule. I bet you're a lot of fun. Wendy, once we're settled in, we may just take you up on that."

Aaron and Stephanie stood a short distance back from the front desk. They were polite and waited to speak with Wendy until the Brenchs completed their check-in.

Once our new arrivals left with the bell captain, Wendy

acknowledged us. "Hey, you three, are you here to return the wheelchair? Would you like me to reserve it for the same time tomorrow?"

Aaron helped Stephanie stand and handed her the cane. "You read my mind. Yes, we would like to use it on our afternoon walk tomorrow, but we have another request. I made a seven-thirty reservation tonight at the Courtside Cafe for Stephanie and myself. Will the chair be available then, or should I rent a golf cart?"

"You're more than welcome to use a golf cart tonight, no charge. No one plays on our course at night, although I have heard of night golf. We don't have the proper lighting for that."

Aaron smiled. "That's very generous. We appreciate that. I know you're going to think I'm a pain, but we'd love to have Max join us. We know better than to feed him any people food. I assume he would need to eat his dinner first."

By the smile on Wendy's face, I was sure she thought Aaron and Stephanie were going on a date. Wendy loved romance, making her an easy read. "Max's schedule is clear but let me give Nate a call to see if it's possible for him to go out at that hour." Wendy went behind the front desk into a small closet-sized private space with a direct line to him. It took all of five minutes for her to return with an answer.

"Max can go. You know, Aaron, he's perfectly capable of jumping on the backseat of the cart. When he has free time, he loves to ride with the groundskeepers. You can pick him up here after seven-fifteen. That will give Nate enough time to feed and walk him. It's four forty-five, so you should have enough time to change and get ready as well. I won't be here at that time, but I'll reserve your golf cart and I'm sure Josh, our night manager, will take good care of you. I'll leave him some notes as to when to expect the golf cart and you."

Stephanie's face lit up. I knew Wendy's news made her very happy. "Wendy, thank you so much. You always make wonderful things happen for us."

I looked at Wendy, who ever since I've known her doesn't like to be the center of attention, as her face flushed.

Stephanie then turned and with her cane walked to the elevator. She waved. "See you later, Aaron and Max, my little angel."

Aaron offered to help. "Stephanie, let me assist you."

She replied, "I'll be just fine."

Aaron remained at the front desk. By his tone of voice, I could tell he was excited about this evening. He became animated, not like his usual serious doctor demeanor. "Wendy, I can't tell you how much I appreciate this." He reached over to shake Wendy's hand. Seeing Aaron this animated was something this dog never expected. He ruffled the fur around my neck. "Meet you here. buddy in just a bit. You are my little cupid."

He touched my head again before leaving.

Wendy giggled. "Max, look at the wonderful thing you've just done. Aaron and Stephanie look so happy. Let's go to Nate's office so he can take you upstairs and get you ready for your first big night out."

Of course, Nate was thrilled when Wendy told him how happy Aaron and Stephanie were to have their first date tonight. He had me jump up, placing my front paws on his lap so he could give me the biggest and best hug ever. I sighed, wishing I could find someone for him. I know who I wanted him to fall in love with. No secret it's Wendy, but that's for another day since I still have to figure out how to make that happen.

Nate, I sensed, was elated that another two of his guests were brought together by his wonderful, adopted dog, blurted out. "In all my days as innkeeper, I never dreamed Max would be a matchmaker, only a great companion to lift my guests' spirits."

"I know. He's wonderful," Wendy responded as she turned to go back to the front desk. "I'd better leave a detailed note for Josh to help make tonight go as smoothly as possible for them."

Nate nodded and got up to take me outside. I loved going out with him. I've been told by some of our single female guests that Nate's so handsome and so nice he could date any woman he wanted. They even called him a "Babe Magnet."

I wondered why he hadn't until one day on a previous walk, he told me. "You know, Maxie, I had the love of my life. Her name was Annie. She was blonde, bright, always had a smile, and was beautiful inside and out. Annie volunteered at a local animal shelter and always reminded me what great pets adopted dogs make. I adopted you in her honor. We went to college together along with your pal Bruce and senior year I asked her to marry me. I didn't have enough money for a diamond ring so I gave her a plastic one I won in a gumball machine and explained that her real diamond would come later. She loved it and said 'yes.'"

His eyes teared up, and he paused to compose himself before he continued. "We were happy until one night as she drove back to campus from her part-time job, a drunk driver hit her head-on and she died. That driver took everything I held precious away from me. It's still difficult for me to think about dating again. I've been introduced to many great women over the years, but our love was so deep, my heart wasn't into it. The Inn now consumes most of my time and I treat my guests like family hoping to make their stay memorable. And then you came into my life and stole my heart. I love you, pal."

No secret here. I loved him too. Tonight's walk was brief, but on our return, I watched a small group of women check Nate out in whispers. Bet they were hoping to get his attention. Once back, Nate took me upstairs for a healthy dinner, a brief rest, and some primping in case any photos were involved. "Max, you're their escort tonight. Who knows? You may be starting another romance? Anyway, we need you to look your best."

He took off my Turtle Inn bow tie and brushed me. He left me for a few minutes to return with a large box of the fanciest bow ties I'd ever seen. He smiled. "Someday, bud, you're going to be in weddings, and I bought these for those special occasions." He pushed some aside to select one. "This baby blue satin bow tie and matching vest will wow them, especially since I overheard Stephanie tell Wendy her favorite color is blue." I loved that and sat up straight so he could put them on me.

"You look so handsome. I'll get your blue leash." He left me again to get my leash before looking at his watch. "It's a little past seven. I'm sure Wendy called the restaurant before she left and gave them my instructions for you."

More instructions? What is Nate up to now?

We went back downstairs. Wendy had gone home, but Josh, our night manager, held down the fort. Josh, a graduate student at Florida Gulf Coast University, wore silver-rimmed glasses which made him look smart, but the glasses and look didn't prevent our women guests from frequenting the front desk during his shifts. He winked as he took one look at me. "Max, you are one cool dude. What the women say about you is true. You are our furry babe magnet."

Of course, I am. Just as Josh finished his compliment, I saw Aaron step out of the elevator, looking dapper in dark-colored Bermuda shorts and a striped collared shirt. By the way he smiled at me, I think he knew he looked good and was ready to wow Stephanie. Not hard to do with his new get-up.

"Thought I'd come down a little early," Aaron told Josh and Nate. "I could pick up the golf cart and get it ready for Stephanie and Max. Were any pink long-stemmed roses delivered for me?"

Josh pulled a long florist box from under the counter. "They arrived about ten minutes ago and are beautiful. Stephanie's going to love them. As for the golf cart, I'll call and have someone drive it to the front of The Inn."

Josh called maintenance as Aaron spoke to Nate. "Thanks for Max. He's the reason Stephanie and I are on a dinner date tonight. We have become very good friends in a short time. Who knows where that will lead? Max came to find me on the tennis court after Stephanie fell. Tonight, I hope to make her forget about her injuries and begin to enjoy a special vacation for as long as she's here."

Aaron turned after we heard Stephanie using her cane come out of the elevator. She looked especially pretty wearing an ankle length spaghetti strap floral sundress and matching shawl. By the look on Aaron's face, she knocked his socks off. The cart arrived and Josh secured the florist box to the back so Aaron could give the roses to Stephanie at the restaurant. Aaron helped Stephanie walk down the ramp as he held onto my leash. He smiled.

"I'm so happy we could share this special dinner

tonight. Nate's letting us use the golf cart and of course Max is with us."

I watched Stephanie take a deep sigh and squeeze Aaron's arm. Stuart, from maintenance was waiting at the bottom of the ramp with the golf cart. My Nate is one sneaky guy. He's such a romantic. The cart was decorated with silk flowers and ribbons. I remember he told me the silk flowers were reserved for weddings, so he must have considered this date pretty special. I watched Aaron assist Stephanie onto the cart and once he let go of my leash, I hopped on the back, careful of the florist box. I loved doing that.

Stephanie looked up at the decorated cart and said, "Aaron, you make me feel like a princess."

Aaron beamed. "You are our princess."

I barked in agreement.

As we rolled away from The Inn, I marveled at how special my new home looked at night. The front portico's hanging lights looked regal as small ground lights on either side of our path lit our way to the restaurant. The tennis courts' overhead lights were bright enough to keep some die-hard tennis players going. Some recognized Aaron and waved.

Stephanie sighed. "It's so lovely in the early evening. I can hear crickets and some birds splashing as they dive for fish in the bay. Thank you again for arranging the cart, the dinner, and Max."

"My pleasure," Aaron responded. "You helped me get over my depression from my cancelled wedding, so I should be the one thanking you." He looked straight ahead. "Well, how about that? Even the tennis restaurant looks better at night with all the multi-colored lights in the shrubs around the patio. Guess I never noticed them before because I always eat earlier and inside."

He parked the cart near the front entrance and helped Stephanie step out. He handed her the cane. Since I was trained to wait, I didn't care how long it took because I wanted them to be happy. Aaron picked up the florist box before he grabbed my leash.

Rachel, our server from lunch, popped out of nowhere and ran to help Stephanie walk inside the screened patio room. She greeted us as she took over Stephanie's care. "Hi, you three. Long time no see. I have a very special table waiting for you. Please follow me." She led us to a quiet section in the very back of the room. "This section is usually reserved for small groups and parties. Since it was empty tonight, Nate reserved this entire section so you can have a private dinner."

That's my Nate, always trying to make things better for his guests and anyone he knows. I only wished he would watch out for himself like that. Stephanie's eyes became as wide as a full moon as she savored the ambiance of the moment. The round table was set for two with a linen table-cloth and fancy flowered linen napkins, not the paper kind I liked to shred in my former life.

"This is just beautiful", Stephanie added as she held up one of the two wine glasses decorated with The Inn's logo.

Rachel noticed how pleased Stephanie was and added, "I'm so happy you like everything. The centerpiece is composed of flowers picked from The Inn's garden while that elegant floral patterned china is reserved for weddings. If you look up, bright colored paper lanterns hang from the ceiling and surround only your table."

I saw Stephanie's eyes light up as bright as the decorations. "Aaron, this is absolutely lovely. You really didn't have to do all of this. And Max, with his special outfit on...I repeat, you two make me feel like a princess."

Stephanie was a princess...my doggy princess. Aaron escorted her to her seat. He put the box under the table before he pulled out the chair to help Stephanie sit. As soon as she did, Rachel took her cane to store during dinner. Aaron then picked up the box, opened it, and held up the bouquet of long-stemmed pink roses. "Stephanie, these are for you. They are as delicate and lovely as you are."

She was overwhelmed and gushed, "They're so lovely! Pink roses are my absolute favorite. Thank you." Aaron kissed the top of her head before sitting down. I remained with Stephanie sitting by her chair.

Rachel returned with the menus. She placed a bottle of wine on the table. "What gorgeous roses. Would you like me to put them in some water for you? I'm sure we have an extra vase."

"That would be very nice, Rachel," Stephanie replied.

Our favorite server continued. "Nate advised me he wanted your evening to be exceptional and would like to buy a bottle of wine to accompany your dinner. He chose his favorite Merlot, but added that you should choose whatever you like."

Stephanie excitedly interrupted, "Merlot is my favorite!"

"Merlot is an excellent choice and a wonderful surprise. How did he know Stephanie and I are both red wine drinkers?" Aaron asked.

Rachel smiled. "Nate wouldn't be a good innkeeper if he didn't know his guests' preferences." She uncorked the wine and poured a small amount into Aaron's glass first.

He smelled its bouquet, swirled the red liquid in his glass, and tasted it. Putting his glass down, he added, "Nate has excellent taste. This is wonderful." Rachel filled their glasses as Stephanie and Aaron perused the menu.

"There are so many delicious choices for dinner, I'm impressed," Stephanie said.

Aaron responded. "I can see that. I usually have a salad and soup or sandwich at night, but there are loads of dinner choices here. I'll have to pay better attention from now on."

Rachel cleared her throat. "If I may, we have a wonderful chef recommended special tonight Chateaubriand for two, served with au-gratin potatoes, fresh green beans with lemon, and a small Caesar salad."

Aaron replied, "That does sound delicious, but give us a couple of minutes to look at the rest of the menu."

Rachel took the roses from Stephanie as I watched them ponder over all the menu choices just as Aaron's cell buzzed. An odd look came over his face as he read the message. Stephanie paused, "Everything all right?"

"Well," he responded, "Beth just sent me another text. This is at least the tenth time in the last few days. Stu left her high and dry. No surprise there. Now she wants to apologize so we could get back together. She thinks that's as easy as turning a light switch on and off."

"And how do you feel about that?" Stephanie asked, concerned.

Aaron responded, "First of all, I don't want her to spoil our special evening. I think she has a heck of a nerve texting me at all hours, but I'm not surprised. There was a time when I wanted nothing more than to be with her, but you helped me forget about all of that. You're the one who makes me happy. You love who I am and not who you want me to be. Now let's toast our evening and forget about all this Beth nonsense."

I watched the way Aaron looked at Stephanie and

sensed he told her the truth. He lifted his glass. "May tonight be the beginning of a long and happy relationship."

Stephanie nodded and clicked her glass to his. "To a very long one. You're just that wonderful." She smiled. "You know that chef's special sounds great. What do you think?"

Aaron waved Rachel over. "I think so too."

Rachel returned with Stephanie's roses in a tall vase and placed them on the far end of the table before taking their order. All I could think was, "Hope they drop some steak." Bad attitude I know, but what can I say, the aromatic smells coming from that kitchen were overpowering.

Rachel left for a few minutes before returning with a serving cart filled with a basket of fresh baked rolls, a silver plate of butter patties shaped like rosebuds, and a large silver salad bowl to mix their Caesar salad at the table. When she finished, she filled two salad dishes and presented them to Aaron and Stephanie, along with the rolls and butter.

Rachel said "Enjoy."

Stephanie responded. "The salad looks so perfect, how can we not?"

My two new lovebirds began to converse in between bites. I remained quiet and listened as Aaron spoke first. "I already explained that the only reason I'm here is because I prepaid for a honeymoon that wasn't meant to be. I thought I would just play tennis and try to repair my broken heart. Meeting you has changed my entire vacation as well as my outlook on life."

Stephanie took some bites of her salad, listening intently. "I'm so sorry Beth treated you like that. You're too nice a guy. But believe me, it was better to break-up before you got married rather than after. Divorce makes a break-up far more complicated. I too came here to forget about my broken heart. Both our hearts needed mending and the best cure is here with us, our handsome furry friend Max, who brings us closer together with each passing day."

She reached down and stroked the back of my neck. "I wish I could take you home, Maxie, but I know Nate would never let you go and I can't blame him."

Aaron took another sip of wine. He placed his glass down and looked into her eyes. "Never realized how badly your heart was broken. You always seemed so together, strong, and happy to me."

Stephanie swirled her wine. "I am happy. When you find out your husband, a powerful and rich Senator has been cheating on you behind your back with some of his rich donors, you are happy to rid that problem from your life for good. Initially it broke my heart. But to stay with him would have been a bigger, more painful mistake."

I saw Aaron mull over what Stephanie said. He added, "In this instance you're right. When Beth and I first dated, we were the center of each other's universe. We could finish each other's sentences. She knew what was involved with my work before she agreed to marry me. I'm a gynecologist and always reminded her that babies do not wait, but she tired of waiting for me and tired of my unconventional schedule. I can't blame her. If the tables had been turned, I'd probably feel neglected too, but she never said a word until a little over a month before our wedding. That's when I learned she met someone else. She was lonely and my best man was there to fill that void."

Stephanie reached for Aaron's hand. "You're such are a sweet and thoughtful guy. Beth doesn't know how lucky she was. And with your best man, no less. What a louse. At least my husband did it with bimbos I didn't know. I guess we've both had our hearts broken, but let's not ruin our evening talking about those two miserable people. How's your salad?"

"Delicious. Especially with those fresh baked rolls I shouldn't eat. The staff is definitely spoiling us." Aaron mused. He looked out the screen nearest his seat. He pointed to three blue herons in the clearing not too far from the patio lights. "Look at those beautiful, tall birds."

As he pointed, a tiny piece of his buttered roll dropped from his hand and into my mouth. Guess I better take good care of The Inn and clean up the crumbs on the patio floor. Yum! Delicious is right!

Once he realized what happened, he said a quick "oops", but it was too late. I swallowed that tiny piece of bread so fast no one ever knew it was there. Stephanie looked at me before checking out Aaron's guilty face. They both laughed before Aaron said, "Have to be quick with this guy. I'll try not to drop anything else. Nate will never allow him to come out with us foodies again."

Rachel arrived to clear their salad plates before returning with our, I mean, their Chateaubriand accompanied by vegetables. By Stephanie's expression, I knew she enjoyed the formal service. Rachel took each dinner plate to the cart and served the carved meat, scooped the au gratin potatoes and fresh green beans with lemon. She served Stephanie first, then turned her attention to Aaron. She asked, "I see that your wine bottle is empty. May I bring you another?"

Aaron took a quick glance at Stephanie. She winked. He responded. "You sure can, we'll have another bottle of the same, but please put this bottle on my bill. Nate already did enough for us this evening with our private table, flowers, and wine to make tonight so special."

"I will, sir." Rachel replied, leaving with the serving cart and returning shortly with the bottle of wine.

I lifted my nose in the air. Oh, the smell of the beef! I felt like rolling over on my back and kicking my legs in the air. Steak! I never had any. Nate was way too strict with me. I know it's for my own good, but at times I feel like I'm still in service dog training. In his defense, he tells me every day about how much he loves me and wants to keep me healthy.

Even so, I hoped a piece of steak would fall right into these limber chops. My face partially hidden by the table-cloth, I waited with mouth wide open as I enjoyed listening to the soft tones of Stephanie and Aaron's conversation. They talked about all sorts of things, like where they grew up, where they went to school, even their past pets.

Aaron looked for me! My head and paws remained partially hidden under the tablecloth, a prime position for scooping. He lifted the tablecloth to see my open mouth and laughed.

"Maxie, you're the best. I would love to give you some steak, but if I did, Nate would never let you come with us again, and we're signed up for two hours tomorrow after-noon. In order to reserve our longer visit, I already had to forgo my morning walk because other guests wanted to share in your magic."

I pulled my head up from under the tablecloth and wagged my tail to let him know I understood.

"Aaron, you didn't have to do that for me," Stephanie interrupted.

"No worries," he responded. "I still have two hours with my two favorite companions." He reached over to touch her hand.

By her smile, I could tell she loved his attention! So did

I. I hoped they would stay together even after their time at The Inn was over. Rachel came back and interrupted their romantic movie moment. She pointed to Stephanie's plate and asked, "Have you finished?"

Aaron chuckled. "Did the clean plates give us away?"

"I'm glad you enjoyed everything." Rachel added as she picked up their dishes. She advised them before she left. "Chef Andre has prepared an incredible dessert for your special evening. He said it's with his compliments."

Wow, these two are sure getting the red-carpet treatment.

Stephanie smiled. "I can't wait to taste it. Please thank him for us."

Rachel disappeared into the kitchen and returned shortly with two covered dishes on her cart. She opened the smaller one first. I smelled something special for me. "This one is for Max. It's a freshly baked pumpkin dog biscuit."

I heard my name, so I sat up as straight as an arrow almost hitting my head on the table on my way up. I looked over to see Rachel holding up three connecting parts of the biggest dog biscuit I'd ever seen. Rachel continued, "Chef Andre looked up a dog biscuit recipe using all natural ingredients and cleared it with Nate. Nate said Max could have one third here and take home the rest in a real doggy bag." She chuckled at her own joke. "The chef already cut it and I will wrap the rest of the cookie to go. This was freshly baked this afternoon."

I couldn't wait any longer. I was drooling. Aaron took the third of the biscuit from Rachel and I gently took it from his hand. "Max, you are spoiled, but I'm glad it doesn't change your attitude."

I lay back down and began to crunch on my treat while Rachel uncovered the second dish.

"Holy cow!" Aaron blurted out. "Holy cow is right. How many cows had to be milked to make all that ice cream?"

Stephanie laughed. "Look at it all."

Rachel explained, "Chef used four scoops of ice cream. Vanilla, chocolate, coffee, and coffee fudge smothered in hot fudge, covered with whipped cream, and served over two eclair shells. I sure hope no one is allergic to chocolate."

Stephanie said, "There have been many times I wish I were. Chocolate is my absolute favorite."

"Mine as well," Aaron added. "Please thank Chef Andre for us."

I looked up as Rachel presented them with spoons. "I will. He'll be so pleased you like it."

We all dug in. Me with my cookie and the two lovebirds with their ice cream. No conversation from this point on. Everyone was absorbed in dessert. Not a peep out of me. I never had a cookie this delicious. I ate it, savoring every bite. Wish I could talk Human. I'd have room service deliver one to me every day. Just kidding, but I hope I receive another one again soon.

The three of us finished our desserts at about the same time. Aaron and Stephanie sat back and took a deep breath. "What an amazing evening," she said. "Thank you for inviting me, for the flowers, the wonderful dinner, and of course for Max."

Aaron whispered softly, "Stephanie, I enjoyed every minute. It was my pleasure."

Rachel came back to clear our dessert dishes and brought Aaron my doggy bag and his bill. Stephanie being considerate, asked, "May I help you with that?"

"No. I'm delighted to treat us. I hope we can do this again soon."

Aaron charged the bill to his room. Rachel took the check and returned with Stephanie's cane. She told us. "Since you left the keys in the golf cart, I took the liberty of asking one of the guys to move the cart closer to this patio door."

Aaron smiled. "That was very thoughtful." Rachel helped Stephanie stand from her chair, picked up the vase of roses, and escorted the three of us through the side door. Aaron carried my cookie box but stopped to remove something from his pocket. He turned to Rachel. "I already added a tip to the bill, but I'd like to give you this extra for your kindness."

I watched Aaron hand Rachel a twenty-dollar bill. Rachel looked surprised. "Thank you. I appreciate this very much."

Rachel then escorted Stephanie to the cart. Once seated, Rachel handed her those special roses as I jumped on the back, ready to head home. As Aaron drove us back to The Inn, I looked up amazed at the millions of twinkling stars that lit up the night sky. I loved staring up at them.

Aaron must have too, because he stopped the golf cart near a clearing close to the water. He turned to Stephanie and said, "You have turned my nightmare of a cancelled honeymoon into a beautiful, starry night. You are one incredible lady. If I'm not too bold, I'd love to kiss you under this exceptional night sky." He placed his arm around her shoulder and leaned in. "May I?"

Stephanie didn't think twice. She returned his embrace with a long kiss.

I lay down on the back of the golf cart, my tail wagging like crazy. I was so happy. Wish I could bark and tell the whole world about Aaron and Stephanie. I watched those two great people kiss for quite a while.

When their last kiss ended, I knew I had to get in on the act. I sat up and leaned over onto their seat to smother their faces with doggy kisses, which made them both laugh.

Aaron gave me a big hug, ruffling my collar. "We love you, Max." I licked them both again. I loved them too.

Aaron cleared his throat, anxious to tell us how we'd spend our two hours tomorrow afternoon. "Okay guys, while I was getting ready for tonight, I had a great idea. The Inn has movies streaming on the rooms' TV's. Since I'm in the bridal suite, I enjoy a large living room with a big screen. We can select a current movie which would be fun for me because it's hard for me to get to a movie theater with my crazy schedule. I can order popcorn, drinks, and snacks from room service and of course, doggy treats for Max. The three of us can snuggle up to a good movie and enjoy a nice, quiet afternoon together. How does that sound?"

Sounded good to me but I don't speak Human. Stephanie blurted, "That sounds wonderful. We won't need the wheelchair, so we should advise Wendy of that. It'll be wonderful to spend a nice quiet afternoon together. I'm happy with any movie you choose Aaron. Seems like it's been a while for me too since I've seen a new movie. Too busy trying to win a Senate race."

I could tell by the ear-to-ear smile that broke out on Aaron's face, Stephanie's response was just what he wanted to hear. "I'll make all the arrangements tomorrow morning with Wendy. A quick kiss and we'll head for home."

The path back was dark, but Aaron took it nice and slow, so I didn't bounce once on the back seat. When we arrived at The Inn, one of the bellmen came running out to pick up our cart. Aaron helped Stephanie out of the cart and escorted us up the ramp. Josh was waiting at the front desk, all smiles. He asked, "And how was your evening?"

"It was like a dream. I felt like a princess," Stephanie blurted out.

"That's wonderful, because that's how everyone here thinks of you," Josh responded as he came out from behind the front desk to take my leash. "I'll let Nate know you're back so he can take Mr. Max for a quick walk before bedtime."

Aaron added, "Please thank Nate for everything he did. He made our evening extra special." Aaron left the rest of my boxed cookie with Josh before he helped Stephanie to the elevator, telling her. "I'll walk you back to your room."

I liked the sounds of that, since I hoped there would be another goodnight kiss. I looked up. My tail wagged so fast my butt wiggled when I saw Nate come down the stairs for me. By the look on his face, he knew how happy I was to see him. I had a beautiful night and hoped more than ever Stephanie and Aaron become more than just friends, but still I was beat. Nate and I went outside for a quick walk before he picked up my cookie box and took me upstairs.

Once home, he took off my fancy duds and filled my water dish. I enjoyed a quick drink, but that drink didn't give me enough energy to play or finish that amazing cookie, not that it was offered. All I wanted to do was crash on my bed. Playing cupid is no easy feat even for me. I drifted off to doggy dreamland, wondering if Stephanie and Aaron shared another goodnight kiss. Guess I'll never know because I couldn't go with them, but I've got my paws crossed.

I carved Z's all night until I heard, "Hey buddy, wake up. It's almost eight. We're late. I let you sleep in as long as possible, but now it's time for breakfast."

Nate rubbed my neck. I rolled over on my back, lifted my legs in the air, and stretched before I yawned a loud yawn. I got up and followed him into our small kitchen. He had my dog food waiting along with fresh drinking water.

I was starving and finished everything in my bowl. Nate put on my Turtle Inn bow tie, and we took our quick morning walk before we checked in with Wendy to see what was on tap for us today.

Wendy was her bright and cheery self. "Good morning guys. You're a little later than usual, but that's okay. You and Max are scheduled to go on a little outing this morning. I already rescheduled his first walk to 12:30."

Outing? Does that mean going in the van? Cool. Where to? I'm happy to go anywhere except to the vet for my shots.

CHAPTER
SEVENTEEN

"**W**here are we going?" Nate sounded a bit annoyed. "You know what a long day Max had yesterday and needs to take it easier today."

I sensed Nate was concerned about my well-being but remained as curious as I was about our destination.

Wendy shook her head. "You do remember that today is The Inn's monthly community service day. You and Max are going to the Whitely Senior Center to meet with its members. Since this is Max's first visit, you'll tell them how he came to live at The Inn and how he helps our guests."

She went on, "I planned ahead and enlarged show and tell photos of his puppy pictures, his service dog training center, his first day here, and even his magic show. I made eight large copies of each. I thought about you giving a slide show, but most of the residents are in their 70's , 80's, and up. I spoke with Mara at the center, and she said they didn't have a big enough TV screen to make it easy for everyone to see, so I thought the photos might work better, If you bring your portable microphone that will help them hear better."

Nate smiled. "Wendy, you're such a great assistant manager, I could hug you." I sighed a deep sigh wishing he would. He shot her an admiring glance. "There are days I don't know what I'd do without you. I love visiting the senior center. I know Max will too."

Wendy beamed back at him. "I bet some of those 'older kids' would like to see a few magic tricks from Max the Magnificent as well. But his job today involves staying by your side and greeting the seniors after the presentation. I've taken care of everything else to make sure both of you have an easier and enjoyable day. The van will be out front to pick you up in a few minutes."

Nate attached my leash, and we went outside to wait for the van. It showed up right on time. The driver was young, handsome, and energetic. He introduced himself. "Good morning, sir and of course Max. My name is Brandon Greene and I'm a brand-new employee at The Inn. I just graduated from technical college and majored in computer science. I am in training to assist in the accounting department. Wendy told me that she would like to have me work in as many different departments as possible, so I'm familiar with them after I move into accounting."

Bet he was hoping to impress Nate. By the smile on Nate's face, he did. Our ride was short but scenic. I always enjoyed the views of tall palm trees and the beach out my side window. We stopped in front of a large, one-story clapboard building. Our van faced the front door.

A pretty young woman in uniform with a name badge came out to greet us. "Hi Nate. That adorable furry guy seated next to you must be Max. Welcome. I'm Mara. I'm the center's program director. Our members are waiting for you in our community room. There are thirty-five of our forty members present. They are very excited.to meet you and Max. This is the biggest turnout for any speaker we've ever had."

And why am I not surprised? Not to brag, but I know Max the Magnificent always draws a huge crowd. We got out of the van and entered their community room to applause. Wow, what great people! They all smiled, happy to see us. Nate and I walked close by the front row so some of the residents could pet me as we walked to the podium that faced the entire group for our presentation.

Nate set up his portable microphone before he motioned for them to stop applauding. "What a wonderful welcome. Max and I are delighted to be here. Thank you for inviting us. My name is Nate Pierson and I'm the innkeeper of The Two Turtles Inn here on Sanibel Island. My sidekick, Max, is our canine concierge who looks quite dapper, I might add, in that turtle bow tie he wears when he's on duty."

Wow! They applauded again, so I sat up straight and gave them my best pose. I heard some cameras click. Nate touched my head to let me know he was about to begin his presentation.

"The story of how Max came to Sanibel and The Two Turtles Inn began a little less than a year ago. This fine young fellow began life in a service dog training facility. He was born there and was the only mixed breed dog they ever attempted to train. Notice I used the word attempted. I'll pass around enlarged photos of the center and of Max as a puppy."

That brought laughter from the audience, anxious to look at the photos. "Unfortunately, or should I say fortunately for us, his overwhelming love of people took him down a different path, one that led him straight to our Inn."

Thanks, Nate, that's a diplomatic way of telling them I flunked out of service dog training school, but he's one consummate salesman who can make anything sound good.

"The training center manager, Bruce, is a college friend of mine. I had already mentioned to him that I was looking for the right dog for this job and he called me as soon as the trainers decided to put Max up for adoption. I always thought a furry friendly concierge would be a fun addition to our staff and trusted Bruce's judgement, so I didn't think twice about adopting him. I left immediately after receiving Bruce's phone call to pick up Max. When I brought him home, Max fit in immediately."

I wagged my tail and smiled my best doggy smile. More camera clicks as Nate continued.

"I'll pass around some more photos of Max on duty." He handed a set of photos to two members on each end of the front row to share with their section. "Max has his own appointment calendar for scheduled walks and quiet time with guests. All arrangements are made through our front desk. His service dog background makes him the perfect companion to those needing canes and wheelchairs. He's a pup of many talents performing magic shows for the kids as Max the Magnificent. Here are the photos of his show as well. Once a month we have an officer from our local animal shelter come to our Inn to inform our vacationing kids about what wonderful pets shelter animals make. Of course, Max serves as his demonstration dog. We instruct them on how to approach an unfamiliar dog, how to hold the leash, and how to care for their dogs. Both Max and the kids love it."

I heard some of the residents chatting as they looked at my photos while Nate paused to take a sip of his water. Wow! He had to quiet them down so we could continue.

"The service dog center uses only golden labs. As you can see, Max is not a golden lab."

More chuckles from the audience. Nate continued, "It's because Max's mom had a fling after breaking out of her pen. She was in heat at the time and met a very fetching mixed breed male, resulting in a litter of eight puppies. Seven of the puppies from that litter were put up for adoption as soon as they were old enough. But the trainers sensed something special about Max. He was such an intelligent puppy they wanted to train him. They tried but as you can sense by his actions, he loves humans too much."

By now, our senior guests were all smiles. Some clapped. Some continued to whisper.

Nate held up my leash. "If anyone would like to walk Max around the room, he's available."

Three people raised their hands. I could see age hurt one of the resident's mobility, so I took it nice and slow with each of them. One, Tom, was so happy, he said, "I haven't walked a dog since I had my pet cocker, Sparky."

Nate glanced at his phone. Once my third walk was complete, he announced, "If there are no more questions or walks, The Inn's van just pulled up with a special lunch and dessert prepared by our chef just for you. Give us a few minutes and Brandon and I will get everything set up."

The seniors' chatter got louder since they were excited about lunch. Can't blame them. I've heard from some of my guest walkers that it's great but expensive to eat at our place. Nate had me remain inside with Mara to visit with the attendees. I just couldn't help myself. There were four ladies sitting together who seemed so sweet, I had to pull Mara over to them.

Sure enough, they gushed all over me like the grandmothers I never knew. As soon as we started our lovefest, the front doors opened. Nate and Brandon entered with trays of fresh fruit, salads, all different kinds of finger sandwiches, and some very fancy deserts. When Mara saw how much I loved the attention of my newly adopted grandmothers, she left me to go bring out paper plates, forks, napkins, and cups for the gallons of sweet and unsweet tea from The Inn.

One of my newly adopted grandmothers pulled Nate aside when he came to get me. "Your Inn is so generous. We all appreciate this very much."

He shot her the sweetest smile and replied, "Ma'am, we are happy to do this for all of you."

Mara then got everyone's attention. "Okay folks, please stay in line by the rows in which you're seated. The Inn brought more than enough for everyone, including seconds, so don't worry that you'll miss out."

Everyone listened to Mara and filed through the buffet line in an orderly fashion. The room then became very quiet as the attendees enjoyed all the goodies. Nate and I worked our way through the group, thanking everyone for inviting us to visit and hoping they enjoyed their lunch. One lady kissed Nate on the cheek. "I miss having a dog, so Max's visit makes it that much more special for me."

Our visit over, we headed back to The Inn. Wendy had a bowl of cold water and a cookie waiting for me, and a bottle of water for Nate. She glanced at her watch, smiling at us. "You two like to cut it close. Max, a new guest wants to take you for a walk. After that, you have a nice break before Aaron and Stephanie come by for their two-hour appointment. You sure are popular. Pretty soon, I won't be able to keep up with your schedule."

Wendy smiled. I loved when she did, so I wagged my tail even though I heard her say before we left that I had an easier day. I didn't mind my busy schedule. I love what I do. As soon as I finished my drink, I heard the elevator doors open. My ears shot straight up because I heard what sounded like wheels on the tile floor. I looked over and saw a beautiful young lady in a wheelchair. Wendy waved her over to the front desk.

"Hi Kate, hope your day is going well." Wendy walked me out to her. "Kate Whiteford, please meet your furry escort, Max, our canine concierge. He'll be your guide for the next hour around the property."

As Kate wheeled herself closer, I noticed she was well dressed, immaculately groomed, and appeared to be in her mid-twenties. With the kindest smile, she said, "Nice to meet you, Max."

She held out her hand, and I gave her my paw. She liked that. "You're quite the charmer, more so than most men I meet." Kate then turned to Wendy. "My friends suggested I get a service dog to help me around my apartment, accompany me on walks, and best of all, be my best friend. When I heard about Max, I wanted to take him for a walk or at least try, anyway. I read his bio. Imagine a dog with his own bio in The Inn's information book. I saw he started training as a service dog so I should be in for a real treat."

Wow. My reputation precedes me. I do remember some of my training with patients using wheelchairs.

Wendy asked right away. "If you think you'll need assistance getting down the ramp, I'll call Mark, our bell captain."

Kate shook her head "no" as her long light-colored curls continued to shake after her head stopped. Wendy sounded a bit skeptical. "Okay, but I'm going to keep a close watch on you two going down that ramp."

Kate reached for my leash. She knew she had to keep it

tight to control me. I licked her hand and made her giggle before she said, "Come on, Casanova, let's go."

She wheeled herself to our front door. Mark opened it and shot a wink back to Wendy. He stood outside and watched us go down the ramp. Kate must have maneuvered ramps before because she knew to take it easy and slow to the front lawn. I kept pace with of her. When we reached the bottom, she looked at me. "Okay, Max, lead the way."

I chose the paved path with a view of the Back Bay and kept us centered so she could enjoy the sweeping scenery. After about fifteen minutes, we stopped our walk and Kate locked her chair. "Look at all those lovely birds," she commented.

I wasn't surprised. Those birds always seem to garnish all the attention away from me and make me jealous.

Kate continued. "Max, you know I haven't felt this good in a long time. My mobility problem happened only a little over a year ago. I went skiing in Vermont and took such a hard fall, people around me thought I wouldn't make it. I was in the hospital for what seemed like forever before I learned I was paralyzed from my right knee down."

I loved my job. Humans confided in me, and all I had to do was listen. It sounded easy, but many of their stories tugged at my heart like Kate's.

She further explained. "I fractured my fibula, which caused nerve damage to the peroneal nerve and affected my ability to lift and therefore use my right foot. At the time, I didn't know the extent of my handicap and became very depressed. I thought my life as I knew it had ended, but my parents and all my friends reminded me how much I had to live for and how much I had to contribute. As soon as I was able, I started physical therapy. That helped build my strength. I was told a good percentage of people like me have some kind of recovery, so I am trying very hard to make that happen. Maybe my walks with you will encourage me to find a service dog to help me progress and one I could love to pieces. I'd love to find a dog as sweet and as smart as you."

Wagging my tail, I licked her hand. Sure wish I could be that dog, but I already have a big job taking care of Nate.

"You know, Max, a husband and kids are on my bucket list, but my future husband will have to be a real patient and understanding guy, not like my former fiancé. He broke our engagement because he said he didn't want to spend the rest of his life taking care of me. Imagine how insensitive that was and how that shattered my heart. My effort to improve will require a lot of work and even more encouragement."

She stroked the back of my neck. I lifted my head to show her I wanted more. I know we just met, but I felt like I've known her for a long time and fell in love with her at once.

"You know," she said, "I recently started speaking to school groups with handicaps about keeping a positive attitude and how that changed my life. I hope to encourage them by telling the truth about my disability while reminding them that they're the same person with the same mental talents they had before they could no longer walk. I tell them to focus on what individual special talents they have to offer others. Your legs are not the only part of your body but trying to convince another with a mobility problem to accept that is easier said than done."

She sighed. "You know, Max, there are many things I miss. I watch others able to stand and dance or practice an easy sport or even climb ten stairs and I get depressed.

Please don't misunderstand. I want them to thrive, but I'm very sad I can no longer do those things."

I watched Kate brush a tear from her cheek before she continued. "I'm sad when other people show pity or sometimes even scorn. You'd be surprised how many people tell me I shouldn't try something new or be part of their group. When that happens, my heart plummets to the deepest part of my body and can't get back in sync. I have to be my own cheerleader and tell myself the same things I tell those kids. Someday soon, I hope to find a dog like you I can take to those meetings with me. I live in Florida, so I'll ask Wendy about your former service dog training center and, after I get home, pay it a visit."

I sure hope she does because my center is one of the top service dog training facilities for special needs in the country. Maybe Kate will get one of my former buddies who unlike me finished their training and will be able to assist her properly. I hope she does that. Now I wondered if I'd met any patient guy Kate might like. I'm sure there must be someone at The Inn who fits that bill. Kate interrupted my thoughts.

"Max, I certainly can yack. Our time has gone by way too quickly. Guess we'd better head back."

I could feel Kate tighten my leash as she unlocked her chair. Our return trip was going along just fine until a tall young man wearing glasses crossed our path reading text messages on his phone. I looked straight at him and barked as loud and as frantically as possible, but he paid no attention. He kept walking and crashed right into us. Surprised since he didn't see us coming, he didn't fall but wobbled bumping into Kate's chair, making her swerve off course and into the bushes. Somehow, Kate remained in her chair which tilted sideways and leaned into those same bushes.

By the tone of her voice, I knew Kate was upset. "You idiot, watch where you're going," she shouted at him. "You could hurt someone."

The tall, muscular young man pushed his glasses up on his nose. "I'm so sorry, miss. I was checking my messages. Pretty lame excuse, especially since I'm supposed to be here on vacation. Please let me help get your chair up and back on the path."

By her refusing to look at him, I knew Kate was miffed. She groaned and shot back. "Not on your life. That's why Max is here to look out for me."

I can understand why she might have been upset enough to refuse help, but she had to understand I'm not capable or strong enough to get both her and her chair back up on this path. I hope she reconsiders, because all I can do is bark or run back to Wendy for help.

She looked straight at me and in a determined voice insisted. "Max, you're going to have to pull as hard as you can to get my chair up and out from the bushes. I'm going to tie your leash to the arm of my chair." Kate did that before shouting. "Ready? Pull Max. Pull as hard as you can."

I tried as hard as I could to move Kate and her wheel-chair back onto the path, but it was to no avail. Her chair was leaning sideways, which made this an awkward even unattainable task; add to that how heavy the chair was with her weight added to it. The wheels were stuck deep into the dirt and pebbles, making my job even more impossible. Thank goodness that persistent young man refused to leave us. I could see her predicament really concerned him as he spoke to her again.

"Please miss, let me assist you. My name is Jeff Black. I guess after what I did to you, it should be 'Jeff Mud' but allow me to get you upright and push you back onto the path."

I watched as Jeff approached Kate. She waved her arms around in the air, trying to prevent him from touching her or the wheelchair, but he was determined to help. "Look, I caused this mishap. It's my responsibility to straighten it out."

Kate again did everything in her power to fight him off but couldn't stop him. Jeff used his muscular arms to pull her chair upright, and with one hard shove, got her back on the paved path. He was out of breath as he looked at Kate. "Once again, please accept my apology."

She refused to look him in the eyes and was not interested in anything he said or did. She offered a curt "Thank you," before setting her wheels in The Inn's direction. Jeff followed us.

Aware he was behind us, Kate turned. "Please go away and leave us alone. I don't want to see you ever again."

When we reached The Inn, Mark, our bell captain, assisted us up the ramp and into the lobby where we saw Wendy standing behind the front desk checking her reservation book. She took one look at Kate and knew something was wrong. I'm sure the tears streaming down Kate's face were a dead give-away. Wendy came running out from behind the front desk and grabbed both of Kate's hands. "Are you all right? You look like you're in a world of hurt."

Kate tried to wipe the tears streaming down her cheeks with her hands. "Hurt doesn't cover how I feel. I'm physically fine. I didn't get hurt that way, but I get so angry when people are rude and insensitive because I'm disabled. They have no idea how hard it is to be unable to help yourself but always need to rely on others, especially if at one time you were 'normal'. My disability makes me feel so inadequate. There are times I don't feel whole, not a complete person. That terrible feeling gnaws at my heart and brain, making me depressed. It's a real downer, one from which it's hard to elevate my spirits, but I manage to make myself do it every time I feel this way. Oh, how I wish that arrogant man never crossed my path. Right now, I'd like to punch that guy out."

I lay down next to her wheelchair, thinking I've seen her arms at work. Darn. She's strong. If I were a betting dog, in that fight, my money would be on her. When I licked her ankle, Kate smiled her first smile since the accident happened. Wendy went back to the front desk to grab some tissues for Kate and handed her some. "What on earth did that man do to upset you so much?"

Kate sniffled. "Some inconsiderate idiot who's staying here named Jeff Black was reading his phone messages and claimed he didn't see or hear us approach. He kept walking and crashed into us, knocking my chair off the path and into the bushes. Max tried his hardest to pull me back on the path but couldn't, so I had to have that horrible person assist me. Ugh! Just the thought of him makes me want to throw up!"

Wendy couldn't help but interrupt. "Did he apologize?"

"Yes, he did, but his apology came a little late in my book. Once on the path, Max and I made it back in good time. I didn't want to keep Max's next walk waiting. Anyway, so you know what he looks like, he's tall, very muscular with short dark hair and was wearing an 'I love Sanibel' T-shirt'. You may want to pass his description on to warn others."

Kate then returned my leash to Wendy. She patted my head. "Love you, little guy. Thanks for sticking by me." With that, she turned and wheeled herself to the elevator.

Kate wiped a few more tears aside as she waited for the elevator doors to open. Once they did, she prepared to wheel her chair inside. To her surprise, Stephanie stepped out slowly using her cane.

I listened hoping Stephanie would sense Kate's distress. Just as I hoped, she stopped to speak to Kate. "Hi. My name is Stephanie Jakes, and it appears that neither one of us could win an Olympic sprint." She smiled that irresistible smile of hers, which made Kate look up at her and grin.

Wow, Stephanie sure has magical powers of persuasion.

"Nice to meet you, Stephanie. I'm Kate Whiteford. I plan on winning one as soon as I complete my physical therapy. Thanks for making me smile. I had a tough morning because of an inconsiderate guest."

Stephanie held her hand out to Kate to shake.

"Don't let it ruin your day. Whoever it was is not worth your time. Think about all the nice guests you've met at The Inn and of course Max."

"I'll shake on that. Max is the best. I'd love to have a service dog like him."

The two women shook hands. Stephanie pushed the elevator button for Kate and explained.

"I came down to pick up a fed ex package from my employer Wendy had called me about earlier. Hope to see you again soon. Perhaps we could have tea one afternoon."

The elevator doors opened. "I'd like that." Kate replied as she wheeled herself inside ready to go back to her room. Stephanie walked to the front desk. Wendy held my leash and still appeared upset by Kate's incident, but managed a smile.

"Hi Stephanie. Please give me just a few moments. I have your package in our locked mail drawer."

Wendy took me behind the counter and opened the mail drawer. She handed Stephanie the thick envelope.

"Thanks for your help Wendy." She then looked at me with her adoring eyes. "See you in just a bit, sweetie." With that, she hobbled back to the elevator.

Wendy whisked me around the counter and filled my water dish. I was so happy she did. By now I was dry as a bone. As I lapped down the delicious cold water, that same man Kate told Wendy about entered through the front door. Good thing Kate was already in the elevator. No telling what she'd do if she saw him. He walked to the front desk and rang the bell on the counter for assistance. Wendy left me to see what he wanted.

"Yes sir. You're Mr. Black, aren't you? How may I assist you?"

"Thank you for remembering my name. I'd like to send flowers to another guest. I went for a walk earlier and was reading my phone messages, not paying any attention to what was going on around me, when I collided with a young woman in a wheelchair. I ran into her pretty hard since I knocked her and her chair off the path, sending it sideways. I'd like her name and room number so I can send her flowers along with a note of apology."

"I hope you can understand, we don't give out guest information without their permission. May I be of help in any other way?"

That's my girl, always trying to avert World War Three while protecting our guests' privacy.

"Maybe you can. If I have the florist deliver them with a note to the front desk, will you make sure she gets them?"

Wendy smiled. When it comes to a possible romance, she's always ready to help. "Why, Mr. Black, that's most thoughtful. Of course, I will."

He nodded, looking at his phone. "Thank you. I found the number for the local florist online. I'll call and make the arrangements from my room phone." I watched him leave for the elevator.

I don't have to go to the movies or the theater for entertainment. The lobby elevator doors work like a stage curtain. With each opening comes a different story and cast of characters for me to get to know. The next time the doors opened, I saw Stephanie using her cane and Aaron helping her walk to the front desk. I couldn't wait to go to the Bridal Suite. Wendy, being efficient, had already pulled the wheelchair from the back.

CHAPTER
EIGHTEEN

Wendy beamed at the happy couple. I know how much she liked both of them since I've only heard her tell me that at least a thousand times. "Hi Aaron and Stephanie, you're clear for two hours with Max. I'll move the chair around the front desk so you can get ready for a fun afternoon."

Aaron blurted out, embarrassed he neglected to tell her. "Wait. Wendy, I'm sorry I forgot to tell you. We won't need the wheelchair." Wendy stopped pushing the chair and turned looking surprised. Aaron explained his plans. "Stephanie won't need the chair today because we're going to watch a movie in my room, I'm in the Bridal Suite and I've already downloaded the film and ordered snacks from room service. All we need to complete our plans for a relaxing afternoon is Max."

Well, didn't that make my tail wag.

Wendy gushed. "What a great way to spend the afternoon. I wish I could join you. Max looks like he's up and ready to go." She took a quick peek in my appointment book. "Max has no other appointments this afternoon, so if the movie runs over two hours, he can stay longer, but he has to be back by five so Nate can take him out and home."

Stephanie laughed. "Gee, Max, it's our lucky day."

Aaron took my leash from Wendy and escorted Stephanie and me to the elevator. I was thrilled since I had never been to the Bridal Suite before. We got off the elevator and walked to two double doors with brass wedding bells over the number. Once inside, I couldn't believe my eyes. Aaron's place was bigger than ours.

He let go of my leash so he could assist Stephanie through the narrow entrance hall and into the living-room. He helped her get comfortable on the couch before he turned on the big screen TV. I snuggled next to Stephanie's feet as Aaron played with some numbers on the remote. Since I couldn't read, I didn't know the title of the movie but once it was set up, he called down to room service asking them to send up his order. Sure enough, ten minutes later, the doorbell buzzed.

Aaron opened the door to let in the attendant with a cart carrying a tray of cheeses, dip and crackers, some strawberries, and of course a giant bowl of popcorn; just my luck all non- dog friendly foods. Two champagne glasses were also on the cart with two silver buckets containing two bottles of the bubbly. The attendant popped the cork on the first one and Aaron handed him a tip before he wheeled the goodies over to where Stephanie and I were sitting.

Once they were alone, Aaron filled the glasses. He and Stephanie clicked glasses as he toasted. "Here's to the most wonderful woman who turned my nightmare into a wonderful dream."

Stephanie liked that and leaned in to kiss his cheek. I sighed happy to see how their relationship improved with each passing day.

Aaron turned the movie on and sat next to Stephanie on the couch. He placed his arms around her. From all the kissing and hugging going on, I don't think either one of them cared what the movie was. I lay there and sighed. I was so happy for the two of them. Aaron kissed Stephanie's forehead and whispered something I couldn't hear in her ear before standing up. "Max, be a good boy and wait here for us. I've got something very special for you."

I thought I smelled a treat in his pocket on the way up in the elevator. He pulled a big dog biscuit from his shorts' pocket and gave it to me before he picked up Stephanie from the couch and carried her into the bedroom and closed the door. She didn't get upset or tell him to put her down, so I could tell she liked what he was doing.

I munched and waited. I could hear their giggles, sighs, and whispers. Before long, they came out of the bedroom. Aaron chuckled. He helped Stephanie sit down on the couch. "How was the movie, Max?"

I wagged my tail and rolled over on my back to get a belly rub, which they both were happy to give.

Aaron checked his watch. Boo Hoo. My time with them must be up. I was right because he said, "Stephanie, it's a little after five. I should get this young man back to his pet dad. Once I'm back, we'll have another champagne toast or two before we get ready to go to dinner." He clicked my leash, and we left to meet Nate. Wish I could hang around longer, especially since they're falling in love.

I was very happy to see Nate, but after we went upstairs and had dinner, I was much too tired to learn any new tricks. I slept like a champ that night, dreaming about Aaron and Stephanie.

The next morning, as soon as I awoke, Nate gave me a big hug. I ate a hearty breakfast, and he fastened my bow tie once I finished. After our morning walk, we went to see Wendy. Nate glanced at me a bit sad. "You know, Max has become so popular, I hardly have time to play with him or take him out for our long walks. Maybe you should add me to his schedule."

Wendy laughed. "You should be happy you have such a popular buddy."

"I'm happy to have both of you," Nate responded before he left for his office.

CHAPTER
NINETEEN

O nce Nate was in his office, Wendy poured water into my bowl. I stopped drinking as soon as my nose sniffed the fragrant breeze wafting into the lobby through The Inn's open front doors. Hmmm… Roses…Gardenias… Mums. It reminded me of how I loved to smell the night blooming jasmine that surrounded my former home. The lovely scent of that jasmine floated through our screened cages every night. Curious, I left my water dish and walked around the front desk to take a peek. Whoa. That was such a huge floral arrangement I couldn't even see who carried it.

Wendy held out an envelope to give to the delivery man. "Thank you. Mr. Black left this gratuity for you." After he left, she smiled as she looked at the attached envelope. "Hey Max, did you have anything to do with this? It's for Kate from Jeff. I've never seen such a gorgeous arrangement. Let me put her name and room number on the envelope and send it up with a bellman. I didn't see her come by for breakfast yet this morning, so I'll call her room to make sure she's in."

Wendy dialed Kate's room as Nate snuck out from his office when he heard me sneeze. I love flowers but my nose doesn't. "How's my ice cream lovin' boy?"

I wagged my tail. I can't lie, the last two days of being concierge has worn me to a frazzle. Tonight, I just want to snuggle on the couch with Nate, eat my doggy ice cream, and watch our favorite TV shows. Nate noticed the flowers when I sneezed again. "Who's the lucky recipient? They're beautiful."

Wendy hung up the phone. "They're for Kate from the young man who crashed into her wheelchair. She doesn't want to see or hear from him again. She's in her room, so I'll call Benjamin to deliver them. Ben's so cute and sweet she'll find it difficult to refuse the flowers and slam the door on him."

Nate went back into his office, shaking his head obviously trying not to get involved. Benjamin's our newest bellman. I liked him too. He's always nice to me, but in a physical conflict, I still would bet on Kate. Benjamin came to the front desk and Wendy advised him where to deliver the flowers.

Since my first walk was late, I waited by the front desk, anxious to see if Benjamin returned with any bruises. It took about fifteen minutes before I finally heard the elevator stop. When the doors opened, I saw Kate wearing a floral sundress and holding that same beautiful arrangement on her lap. It was hard to differentiate where her dress stopped and the flowers began. She adjusted her chair and wheeled herself over to the counter. "I want to send these flowers back. My room attendant helped put them on my lap. The flowers are gorgeous, but not the guy who sent them."

Wendy scurried out from behind the front desk. "But

Kate, they're so lovely. Certainly, you can accept his apology through these flowers."

Kate huffed as she held the flowers up in Wendy's direction. "No, I will not. I'm giving them to you since you've been so nice to me and in fact everyone who stays here. Besides, while I'm here the only guy I want in my life is Max."

Heard that before. Since I was loose, I walked over to Kate. Wendy looked frustrated, unable to respond. As I licked Kate's wrist, she balanced the flowers in Wendy's direction.

"I didn't mean to put you on the spot," Kate said. "I left a message for that man telling him thanks, but no thanks. He was rude and I will not put up with that. The arrangement is beautiful, but so are you inside and out."

Kate struggled again to lift the arrangement onto the counter. Wendy saw Kate's hands shaking. They weren't stable enough to balance that large flower arrangement, so she rushed to help. After rescuing the flowers from Kate's shaky hands, Wendy lifted them onto the registration desk and looked at Kate.

"I'll take good care of them and appreciate your kind thoughts, but I'll send them back to your room after your walk with Max."

Wendy went back around the counter for my leash. Before she could get to it, the front door opened and in came Jeff, all sweaty and hot from his morning jog. He saw Kate and his face lit up like it was on fire. I winced, thinking he was about to take his life in his hands merely by walking over to her. He noticed the flowers on the front desk.

"I see the florist delivered the flowers I sent. I wasn't sure of the right way to apologize, so I called Mom for advice. She said flowers are always a most thoughtful way to do that."

I watched Kate ignore him, holding out her hand for my leash. She turned to Jeff. "Your mom must be incredible to put up with an unfeeling, inconsiderate son like you."

I thought that wasn't a nice response, but it's something. At least she's talking to him.

He appeared to shrug her insult off, trying to be nice. "You're taking Max for a walk? May I join you after I shower and change?"

I could have answered that question myself but had to give Jeff points for persistence.

After a curt "No, we don't have that much time," Kate wheeled herself to the front door.

Wendy called out to her, "Be careful. Are you sure you don't need help?'

Kate ignored everyone and asked Mark to open the front doors. Down the ramp we went. When we reached the lawn, Kate led us to a path heading toward the dock. "Let's go watch the dolphins play. Max, when we get there, you can bark at them all you want, and it'll be our secret."

Now, that's my kind of guest. We made our way to the bench with the best view of the Back Bay. Besides the great view, we preferred that bench because the surrounding pavement was wider and easy for Kate to access her wheelchair. Once she found the perfect spot, she locked her chair, and I sat next to her with my head on her lap. She placed her hand on the very top of my head and stroked my fur as we studied all the ripples in the water to see if any were large enough to hide a playful dolphin ready to surface.

"Max, I bet everyone you meet tells you this, but like I said before, I'd love to take you home. I know that's impossible, but ever since I met you, you made me realize how much a service dog would help me in my daily life."

Just then, we heard a big splash. On cue, I sat up and barked to draw my sea friend closer. A beautiful large silver dolphin did a flip right in front of us before he lifted his head and looked straight at us. "How beautiful," Kate gushed. I could tell by her look of awe she was pleasantly surprised by his visit.

I remember overhearing a guest tell Wendy that dogs and dolphins share a close affinity. Some scientists believe dolphins can hear us bark under the water and the noise attracts them to us. Dogs can hear dolphin sounds under the water as well. If the dolphin senses a dog nearby, he shows his kinship by jumping up or swimming with his fin in and out of the water. I think our new friend knew how I felt about him because he swam in front of where we sat a little longer before he headed further from shore and jumped totally out of the water. Kate laughed and clapped. She was so happy.

"Max, he's amazing! Look at him. He's flipping a fish." That dolphin played with his dinner before he caught it, swallowed it, and disappeared into deeper waters. After our dolphin show, Kate patted my head and mused, "What a wonderful day!" She suddenly became pensive. "Anyway, Max, I know you're smart enough to understand why I didn't want those flowers. After Jeff was so rude and careless, I never want to see him again."

There may be a glimmer of hope in her last statement. We may be making progress since she called him Jeff and not "that man." She continued, "No matter where I go, I meet careless people like him. Some think it's just fine to push a person with disabilities out of their way, physically or verbally. I don't need them in my life."

I sat there thinking, I hope she doesn't think that of Jeff. He was careless and clumsy but not mean-spirited. Anyone who felt that guilty about an accident couldn't be mean. Besides, they are both attractive, smart, and about the same age so if Kate could forgive him, who knows where this might lead?

Just like matchmaker magic, I heard someone coming down the path in our direction. I turned to look. It was Jeff walking at a fast but steady pace. When Kate heard footsteps, she turned and pointed a finger at him. "Don't you dare come near me."

Jeff stopped, surprised by the angry tone of her voice. He looked as oblivious as ever when he responded. "I had no idea you were down here. I thought you might have taken Max down another path. I hope you accepted my apology and liked my choice in flowers. I noticed they were still at the front desk. Didn't Wendy send them up to your room?"

Kate turned her gaze away from him as he continued. "About our accident, again I truly am sorry. I meant you no harm. My friends tell me all the time to pay attention to my surroundings. I try as hard as I can, but I still have mishaps."

After listening to their banter, I felt like saying, "Come on kids, kiss and make up," but since I couldn't talk, I nudged Kate's leg.

She turned her back to Jeff when he pleaded. "Please Kate, I'm really a good guy. You can tell how dense I am because I didn't see you two sitting here."

Jeff took a deep breath and walked close enough to pet me. What's this? Kate pushed his hand away. That's my head, so I shook it to let Jeff know he could continue. He looked at Kate. "Max is not your dog. He's The Inn's. Somehow, I don't think I'm the mean one here."

Kate answered begrudgingly. "Okay, pet him. Max will probably hate it."

Jeff continued to pet me. I nuzzled his hand, hoping to show Kate he's not as terrible as she thinks. Jeff walked around the back of Kate's chair.

"Are you going to push me into the water?" Kate asked with a smirk.

Jeff looked surprised. "What kind of a question is that? No. I'm going to take a break from my walk and join you." He sat on the park bench and inched his way closer to her chair. "May I tell you a little about myself?"

Kate shook her long curls negatively.

But Jeff continued his end of the conversation. "When I'm home, I spend my free time as a volunteer because I love to help people and animals. Right there, that proves I can't be the callous person you think I am. I graduated from law school two years ago and passed the Florida Bar exam. I work as a lawyer for legal aid in Collier County, Naples, Florida. We help people with all sorts of problems, landlord, civil rights, medical, you name it. I don't earn as much as I could in the private sector. Most times I take cases pro-bono, but since I'm single, it's the right time for me to do this. When I have more responsibilities, I'll have to earn more money, but I'll stay on as a part-time volunteer."

He cleared his throat. "My hobbies when and if I have time are running and volunteering at a local Naples animal shelter. I take care of the shelter's day-to-day needs and use my website to find their residents permanent homes. That's me in a nutshell. In case you haven't figured this out, my cell is my doom. I read news, get messages, listen to music, and take photos and videos. Before our accident, I received a message from the shelter that Apricot, a nine-year-old dachshund, needed to find a home ASAP or she'd be put to sleep. I had to e-mail three people who might be able to rescue her, so when we collided, I was combing through my e-mails to find that one of them did."

Kate interrupted, "How do I know you're telling me the truth?"

I saw the surprised look on his face when Kate questioned his integrity. He responded immediately. "Why would I lie about Apricot? I didn't see you the day of our accident. I was consumed in saving this beautiful dog's life. I am truly grateful I found a young couple to rescue her just in time. They love to run and so does she, so it's a match made in doggy heaven. That was the e-mail I was reading when we collided. My mind was hundreds of miles away. I apologize again for my clumsiness. Anyway, the couple who adopted Apricot already had seven other dachshunds, so Apricot has a lot of new friends and good care."

Jeff impressed me. How could anyone be mad at a guy whose purpose was to help animals, especially rescue dogs like me? Jeff reached in his pocket and took out his infamous phone. "Would you like to see photos of Apricot with her new family?"

What's this?

Kate nodded. "Only so I can verify your story."

Jeff moved in closer to her and flipped through his photos. "There's my girl. Pretty isn't she?" He handed the phone to Kate, who looked at the photo of Apricot. Jeff flipped to the next photo of her with her new family.

"I'm sorry again, but I had to save her life. I played with her at the shelter and fell in love with her. Please understand and accept my apology."

Kate remained silent for a minute. "I guess I'm the one

who should apologize. You're not like all those rude people who push me aside on purpose. Yours was an honest though very clumsy mistake. I'm touchy about having to use a wheelchair. My mobility problem stemmed from a fracture. I'm in physical therapy and there is hope. If I work hard, I might not stay wheelchair bound. You said you worked in Naples. Guess what? I live in Bonita Springs just a few miles up the road."

Jeff smiled. "It is a small world sometimes. I'm glad to hear you're on the mend. Say I noticed the floral arrangement was still at the front desk. Why didn't the bellman take the flowers up to your room?"

Kate flushed from embarrassment. "He did, but I was so angry I brought the flowers back and told Wendy she could have them. She said I should reconsider my decision."

Jeff took a deep breath. "Since you know why our accident happened, would you accept the flowers and my apology?"

Kate smiled. "I will."

Jeff was quick to respond. "Well, let's call Wendy and let her know that."

He called from his cell and placed the call on speaker so he could hold the phone in front of Kate. She took charge at once. "Wendy. Jeff explained how everything happened and I accept his apology."

Wendy replied, "That's wonderful. I'll have those gorgeous flowers sent back to your room. I'm glad you two are on talking terms. Jeff seems very nice."

Kate responded with a smile, "He is."

I'm glad I overheard their conversation. That made me happy for them. Jeff and I waited until Kate was ready to head back to The Inn. She was about to take hold of my leash when Jeff asked, "May I accompany you back?"

Kate responded with a happy glimmer in her eyes. "You sure can." With that, the three of us headed back. No surprise, Jeff was a total chatterbox the entire way, identifying some of our local birds and every flower along our path. Kate and Jeff seemed to have a lot in common. Jeff pushed Kate's chair up the ramp. When we reached the porch, she said, "I have Max scheduled for a walk tomorrow morning at eleven. Would you like to join us?"

Jeff smiled. "I sure would. You don't have to ask me twice. Maybe after our walk we could grab lunch at the tennis restaurant, my treat."

Kate laughed. "Sounds like fun. I'll be sure to take it easy on breakfast. I'm trying not to gain any weight. It's hard with so little exercise. We can ask, but I don't think Nate will let us take Max to lunch with us."

Jeff smiled. "Maybe not, but as the old saying goes, if you don't ask, you don't get."

That made Kate giggle. She's so cute when she giggles. From the smile on Jeff's face, I think he agrees. With that, we walked back to the front desk where Jeff left me with Wendy before he wheeled Kate to the elevator. The flowers were gone. I'm sure Ben delivered them to her room again. I took a break from my water bowl to peek around the front desk to see Kate and Jeff get into the same elevator. Wish I could go with them.

I'm proud that I've become a regular doggy cupid. Not exactly how Mom wanted my service dog training to work, but I do help people heal broken hearts, find new love, and become happy again.

I drank my water and had a cookie to get energized for my next walk. Wonder how Stephanie and Aaron's private date went without me last night?

It didn't take long to find out. Especially after I saw how

happy they looked as they walked to the front desk. Aaron kept his arm around Stephanie's waist. I'm sure he told her in his doctorly voice it was to help her balance, but I think he enjoys holding her. Stephanie shot loving glances at him as Wendy pulled out the wheelchair. "Wendy, we think you're amazing," Aaron said as he assisted Stephanie into the chair.

Stephanie added." I met a young lady in a wheelchair yesterday. If it's The Inn's chair, she probably needs this more than I do. So please give her priority. I can use my cane."

That's my Stephanie, always thinking of others. Wendy smiled. "Stephanie, that's very thoughtful. She does need a wheelchair but has her own."

Aaron studied my tired demeanor. "Max looks beat. Is anything wrong? Is he feeling okay?"

Wendy smiled. "I think Max had a bit of a rough go on his last walk, but I'm sure you and Stephanie will cheer him up."

I watched Stephanie pull a little blue bag from her purse and jiggle it in the air. She laughed. "This might work."

CHAPTER
TWENTY

I knew what was in that bag and tried as hard as I could not to drool. Just the thought of that doggy cannoli made my heart pound and my tail wag like crazy.

Stephanie noticed my mood change. "Good boy, Max. Like Mom always said, 'Nothing beats a great dessert.'"

Her mom was right about that. I watched Aaron become impatient. "All right team, enough with the small talk. We are off but not running." He chuckled at his own joke.

Maybe enough conversation for him but not me. I could listen to Stephanie talk and eat a cannoli all day. Aaron walked us down the ramp and onto the path. He surprised me when he chose a different direction, a path that paralleled the road to The Inn. We had a beautiful view of the Back Bay. He spotted a bench under a shade tree and settled us down. Aaron helped Stephanie off her chair and onto the bench. I kept hoping my cannoli would appear soon.

Aaron asked, "Are you two okay here?"

I lay at Stephanie's feet and wagged my tail, watching the pelicans dive bomb for fish. If we're lucky, we might see a couple of dolphins swim close to the seawall. I loved watching them jump.

Stephanie beamed. "This is so wonderful. I miss being able to go down by the water. It's difficult to walk on the pebbled path and dirt near the bay with a cane. If you'd like to walk nearer the water, Max and I are perfectly content to wait here."

Aaron took her hand. "I can't think of anything better than being here with you." He nodded. "And Max of course."

I watched Stephanie dig that blue bag out of her purse and snap my doggie cannoli in half. I sat up so fast I thought my back would snap just like that cookie. She gave me my treat. I savored everything about it. The smell of the filling and the crunchiness of the outside shell put me in a happy trance.

Aaron laughed. "Max, I can see the way to your heart is through your stomach."

Ain't that the truth?

All of a sudden, Aaron pointed to the water. "Look over there! There's a huge ripple on top of the water. Much too big for a dolphin. Wonder if that's what's called a shadow?"

I looked straight at that ripple and barked. I know I'm supposed to behave and stay quiet, but I knew what was under that shadow and wanted them to swim in closer to us. I barked louder.

Aaron looked at me like I was crazy. "You okay, Max?"

As soon as I stopped, we heard loud splashing. Sure enough, a pair of manatees emerged from their shadows and swam in closer. At first glance, we could only see their backs, but as they approached, they played and leaped over each other, often sticking their snouts out of the water for air.

I saw other people walking along the path stop near us to get a closer look. Aaron helped Stephanie stand. "Look at those manatees. I've never seen one outside of an aquarium."

Stephanie added. "I've never seen one at all, only photos on-line."

Aaron continued. "You know, Stephanie, in ancient Native American legends, manatees were believed to be the protector of mermaids; while other cultures thought manatees were mermaids themselves. I read in some African legends, manatees were believed to be once human and chose to live in the water to protect those waters for humans."

By the look in Aaron's eyes, he shared Stephanie's amazement at seeing these wonderful creatures. "In 1492 Christopher Columbus recorded the first sightings of manatees in North America after he caught a glimpse of three. Often referred to as Sea Cows, they are vegetarians who like to munch on sea grass. Whales and manatees both possess shadows that indicate their location under the water."

I continued to bark as the manatees played for at least ten more minutes before swimming off. I could see how astonished Stephanie was by their visit. Aaron put his arm around her and gave her a squeeze before helping her sit down again.

"I've never seen a manatee before. That was absolutely spectacular," Stephanie gushed.

"Just like you." Aaron replied. He hesitated for a minute before announcing. "I thought we'd do something different this afternoon. I already cleared this with Wendy and Nate. The gate to The Inn is not too far from here. To the left of the entrance is The Blue Cow-The Best Homemade Ice

Cream on the Island. If you trust my driving," he snickered, "we can go there and see if the ice cream is as good as they say. We'll have to keep Max close to us because The Blue Cow is near the road. I heard from a good source, they even have doggy ice cream."

Doggy ice cream!

Two great treats in one day! I love it.! That's my kind of afternoon. Say 'yes' Stephanie. Please, oh please.

"That sounds like fun. Let's go. I'm excited," Stephanie answered.

Yeah. Let's go. Can't wait for my ice cream.

"We'll need to leave soon in order to make all this work in two hours. We already put a half hour on our Max clock. Max should love our visit since Nate gave me the okay earlier for him to have a small cup of vanilla."

Cheers! I'm in. Hurry up. Let's go before I start to drool.

Aaron wheeled Stephanie to the front entrance of The Inn with me by his side. All along the way, I felt a cooling breeze coming off the Gulf. The attendant at The Inn's front gate smiled and gave me a pat before waving us through. Aaron made a sharp turn to the left, and we walked less than half a block along the road before seeing a Big Blue Cow cut out of wood with the restaurant name painted on its body. I know that sign well since Nate and I visit regularly. That's where I had my first cup of doggy ice cream. I wonder which flavor I'll choose today. Just wishful thinking since Nate already chose vanilla. Guess he feels vanilla is the safest for me.

I looked at the one-story building with a colorful border of cows painted around its exterior. There was indoor seating, as well as tables outside in a screened room.

As we approached the screened room, a pretty server with braids and ribbons welcomed us. She wore an apron with cow faces on it that matched the sign. "Welcome to the Blue Cow. I'm Sue. Our desserts are guaranteed to give you a moo-ving experience. Please follow me to an outside table since I see you brought our favorite dog, Max." Sue then escorted us to a table away from the road before adding, "Less noise and less dust here."

Stephanie was curious about how Sue knew me and asked. "You know Max?"

Sue leaned down to pet me. "Nate's our landlord. My husband and I own the restaurant. We rent our building from The Inn. Nate brings Max in for doggy ice cream regularly. Nate, who is wonderful to us, loves our Double Dutch Chocolate."

Sue left to help some other customers. Aaron helped Stephanie out of the wheelchair and onto a patio chair.

How about me? I'm pretty wonderful too. Whenever I visit, I sit up straight so customers can pet me. Sue returned with two huge menus. "Nate only allows Max to have vanilla. If you want to see a cute photo, look at Max's on page three of the menu."

Aaron already knew about the vanilla, but that comment sealed my fate. Darn, my gig was up. I was hoping for cherry vanilla. Sue handed out the menus. "Please take your time. We have quite a large selection, so there's a lot to look at besides Max's photo."

I knew about the menu. It was shaped like a cow's head and had four pages. Aaron advised Stephanie, "Let's skip the sandwiches and go straight to the desserts. Wow! Look at this!" He blurted out, "Forty flavors! This is definitely my kind of place. Look at that picture of The King Kong, their massive banana split. I bet King Kong himself would love to eat one."

Stephanie laughed. "I see the picture of the King Kong

but the one of Max, 'Sanibel Island's Best Dog' is adorable. How cute is that? The doggy flavors are listed under his photo."

Aaron turned the page to my photo and smiled. "Great pix, Max."

Stephanie continued, "A banana split? I haven't had one of those in years. In junior high, three of my friends and I would share one once a month after class and it wasn't as big as Kong."

Aaron winked. "Feel like sharing one now? It comes with four flavors, a banana, cherries, whipped cream, and nuts with hot fudge poured over two flavors and caramel over the other two."

Stephanie and I watched a server bring one to a couple whose table was not too far from ours. Stephanie blurted, "Look at how large those scoops are." She pondered the idea for a few seconds before responding. "Sure, let's try one. Why not? We're on vacation."

Aaron became animated. "That's my girl. Now you pick your favorite two flavors and I'll pick mine."

"Sounds like a plan." Stephanie responded just as Sue returned.

Sue flashed a big smile. "Are you ready to order?"

"We sure are," Aaron advised. "We're sharing your jumbo banana split with one scoop of chocolate ice cream and one of coffee. Stephanie, what are your two?"

"I'll have pistachio and mint chocolate chip."

"Stephanie is having a green moment," Aaron joked. "Would it be possible to put the hot fudge on the chocolate and mint chocolate chip and the caramel on the other two and we'll need two spoons, please." He chuckled. "Can't spoil our appetites for dinner and please don't forget Max's vanilla in a dish. Oh, and two glasses and a cup of water for our buddy, please. Thank you."

Sue smiled at Aaron's exuberance and left with their order.

Stephanie giggled. "I feel like a schoolgirl again." She reached over and touched Aaron's hand. "Thank you for making what's left of my vacation so much fun."

I had to sneak my head under Stephanie's arm to make sure I got some attention as well. They both laughed and petted me. It didn't take long for Sue to return with our waters. Mine was in a special plastic bowl that had my photo on it. As she placed it on the floor next to our table, she told us, "These bowls are available at the check-out counter if you know of any pets needing souvenirs."

Aaron chuckled. "Hope you're getting royalties, Max."

Sue responded. "From the very first moment we met Max, we knew he would be a star. We asked Nate for Max's photo and permission to use it in our advertising. We assured him that all profits from the sale of the dishes would go to our local animal shelter as well as ten per cent of our doggy ice cream sales. The Inn's photographer provided that sweet photo of Max. We used an online printing company who rushed our order for the bowls and reprinted our menus. They sell like crazy."

Sue smiled and gave me a hug. She left for a few minutes only to return with my vanilla and their mountain of a banana split and two spoons.

I lapped my ice cream slowly. The first time I had doggy ice cream with Nate, I wolfed it down so fast, I got a brain freeze. I have better manners now. In between licks, I watched Stephanie and Aaron each take a spoon and chow down their dessert feast. They ate six spoonfuls before either of them said a word, but they did shoot some pretty loving looks at each other. Their lack of chatter told me how much they enjoyed their treat.

Normally a chatterbox, Stephanie couldn't restrain herself any longer. "Yum and yum. The caramel goes great with the pistachio and the fudge is wonderful with the mint chocolate chip. This is the most delicious dinner I've had in ages."

Aaron looked into Stephanie's eyes. "You know you made me believe there's life after my break- up with Beth. I'm having such a great time with you I hope it never ends."

"Me too. And to think, Max made this all happen."

"Say, would you like to go for a moonlit walk tonight? Heard you can see a million stars on a clear night. It's supposed to be clear tonight. We can take the path by the road around dusk and if we have digested our banana split by then, we can stop in at the tennis bar for a nightcap after we take in those stars. I read in the room schedule they have a jazz trio tonight. We can listen to music and have a drink."

Stephanie paused. "That would be wonderful, but you don't have to feel sorry for me."

"Who said I felt sorry for you? I enjoy our time together more than you know. I'll ask Wendy if we could reserve the wheelchair. The biggest downside is I don't think Max can come tonight. We've been hogging his attention a lot this week."

Stephanie petted my chin. "I understand, but I just love this little guy."

I sighed a deep doggy sigh at that thought as Aaron signaled for the check. Sue brought the check, amazed all three of us clean plated our ice cream. Aaron helped Stephanie back into the wheelchair and the three of us waddled and rolled ourselves back to The Inn.

CHAPTER
TWENTY-ONE

W e returned a little late. Nate paced by the front desk. He worried about me too much. I know I can't stop him because he does it out of love. Aaron and Stephanie thanked Nate before the two of us took our evening walk and headed home for dinner. I was too exhausted to eat my dogfood, never mind stuffed by all those delicious treats and ice cream. But I persevered and ate enough so Nate wouldn't think I was sick. He finished his tuna salad sandwich before we headed into our small living room that had a TV screen almost as big as the room.

As usual, we both fell asleep watching TV. I can't think of anything better than falling asleep with my head on his arm. Nate woke me up from a sound sleep. It was still night, so he cajoled me into my bed. I went into our bedroom. We were still a bit droopy and both slept until seven-thirty, when Nate's alarm went off.

Morning routine done, we walked to the front desk to see what my schedule held today.

Wendy gave me my morning hug when I heard the elevator doors open. Aaron carried his tennis racket and wore his usual mismatched tennis outfit. Nate greeted him before dashing into his office. He left guest chit-chat, though important, to Wendy because he said it interfered with his work.

Aaron, a natural chit-chatter, stopped to talk with Wendy. "This is the best vacation I've ever had. I'm so relaxed and Stephanie is so much fun. Last night, we made it to the tennis restaurant to listen to the jazz trio and have a glass of wine. We talked for hours. I'm a bit sleepy but hope a round of tennis will wake me up."

Hmm. Sounds like my two new lovebirds had a late night. Wonder how it ended?

Aaron left waving to me. "See you later, buddy."

I wagged my tail, surprised to see Mrs. Forrester at the front desk. "I'm here to take Max for a walk sans my boys. My selfish treat. I love this little guy. I usually walk alone in the morning to clear my mind, so this should be fun."

Wendy handed her my leash. "Have a great time."

Surprised, she took me for a very brisk walk, almost a jog around the longest path much too fast for any chatter. We returned early and since I had a few minutes until my next walk, I lay on my concierge bed trying to sneak in some extra shut eye. Thank goodness I did because I awoke to, "Okay Max, it's eleven, time for Kate and Jeff."

I sat up and shook myself. I'm glad they made peace. I saw Kate and Jeff smiling as Wendy walked me around the front desk to fasten my leash. She sighed, advising them, "He's still a bit tired from yesterday. He had a long day, so please take it easy with him." That's my Wendy, always my overprotective doggy mom.

Jeff and Kate nodded. Jeff said, "We're so happy Max could join us for lunch. We won't overwork him and thanks for giving us two hours with him, especially since it was a last-minute request."

Wendy was polite but firm. "We're glad we could make this work for you. Nate wanted me to remind you not to feed him any human food or give him any human drink. He's got a busy schedule today. Besides, we don't want him to get sick."

Jeff looked at me as I yawned. "Not a problem. We're going to walk to the restaurant, have a light lunch, and listen to their afternoon jazz concert. We're both lovers of jazz and are really looking forward to it. We don't walk fast and once we're there, he can rest under our table while we eat."

Sounds like a perfect afternoon to me.

Wendy interrupted my thoughts. "Thank you so much for that. Oh, and before I forget, no dog cookies of any kind. Something spoiled his dinner last night and Nate has a strong suspicion it was Blue Cow doggy ice cream and biscuits from the doggy bakery."

Jeff lifted his right hand. "Word of honor. No treats of any sort."

He took hold of my leash and off we went. We took our time walking to the tennis restaurant. Kate loved to look at the birds, especially the coral feathered Rosetta Spoonbills along the way. Once there, Jeff wheeled Kate inside the screened patio. Harry, our server, greeted us and found the perfect outside table close enough to enjoy the jazz group yet far enough away so as not to hurt my ears. "When Wendy made the reservation, she mentioned Max would be with you, so I held the best table for your listening pleasure without causing pain to Max's hearing. Dogs hear at a more intense rate than we do. Would you like to start with a glass of wine?"

"Yes. Thank you." Jeff beamed. "Kate, I'm so glad we could do this. I think we should celebrate."

Kate agreed, as Jeff asked Harry for the wine list. I put my head on Kate's feet. I knew she liked that because it made her giggle.

"Harry, please bring us two glasses of the Oregon pinot noir while we peruse the menu."

Harry nodded and headed to the bar as Kate and Jeff read through all the delicious food I can't but would love to have. Kate said, "The open prime rib sandwich with a side Caesar salad looks good to me."

Me too, I thought.

Jeff responded right away. "Let's make that two." He signaled for Harry and gave him "our" orders.

If I'm lucky, maybe some prime rib will drop on the floor.

Jeff held Kate's hand. "You know we don't live far from each other. Maybe we can see each other after we get home."

Kate smiled. "I'd love that. When we collided, I was down on dating and tired of rude men. My selfish ex-fiancé broke up with me right before I arrived here. He said he didn't want to marry someone who needed constant care. Imagine that! I can take care of myself."

Jeff nodded and music interrupted their conversation. They ate lunch and finished their wine. After the end of the first set, we headed back to The Inn. Kate waved her hand in the air, signaling for Jeff to stop. "I just wanted to say thank you for this amazing afternoon. I felt normal again. No one stared at me, made snide remarks, or whispered when I went by. I would like to see you after we get home, but first I'd like to treat you to lunch tomorrow. There's a pizza place right off the Inn's property. It's small, but I've had their delivery and it's very good. Would noon work for you? How does that sound?"

Jeff responded, "Noon would be perfect. Any time is perfect as long as I'm with you. Your ex doesn't know what he's missing, but his loss is my gain."

Jeff sighed. "I have something extra special planned for tonight but I'll have to get Nate's approval." He leaned down and kissed the top of her head. "A two-hour dinner date with Max at the tennis center. They are featuring a blues band. I hope you enjoy different kinds of music like I do. We can still do lunch tomorrow."

Kate giggled before she expressed her approval. "How perfect! I love all kinds of music and we're practically spending the entire day together and with Max."

As we walked back, I noticed Jeff had a new bounce in his step, obviously thrilled she accepted. Wheeling Kate back to the front desk, he handed me over to Wendy. "Please thank Nate for Max and his extra time with us. He's always great company and makes everything fun. We're both crazy about him." He then leaned over and petted my head. "See you later I hope, buddy."

That last comment didn't surprise me since I'm crazy about everyone. Jeff turned to Wendy. "We'd like to make another appointment with Max for a two-hour dinner date this evening, if possible."

Wendy, always happy to assist a budding romance, checked my appointment book and responded, "Seven might work with Nate's approval."

Jeff smiled. "We'd appreciate that and will make our restaurant reservation with that in mind. Thank you."

CHAPTER
TWENTY-TWO

W endy snuck me a small peanut butter treat. It wasn't prime rib, but tasty, nonetheless. Nate likes to buy small cookies hoping to keep me trim. That's fine with me because any cookie is a good cookie. Besides, I'm sure Stephanie will have a doggy cannoli for me later. Just as I swallowed the last crumb, Stephanie and Aaron walked arm in arm to the front desk laughing.

Wendy smiled her sweet smile. "Hi guys. You two look so happy! Max is here waiting. How did you enjoy the jazz trio last night?" She winked at Aaron because he already told her about it.

Stephanie grinned. "The trio was wonderful and the appetizers amazing. I had shrimp wrapped in bacon, and Aaron had Asian barbeque wings over thin noodles. Of course, we shared, but what a great place."

"Wonderful. I'll let Nate know about your experience. He always likes to get feedback." Wendy handed Aaron my leash. "Here's Max. Where are you three going today? You have two hours reserved. Will you need the wheelchair?"

Stephanie shook her head 'no', but Aaron intervened.

"That might be a good idea. It's a bit of a walk. Save your leg, so your fracture can heal."

Now, they're beginning to sound like a real couple. Wendy rolled out the wheelchair as Aaron remarked, "I hope Max isn't too tired for a long walk. I learned last night there is a small shopping center with local arts and crafts stores and a French bakery that serves light sandwiches on the other side of the guard gate across from The Blue Cow. Thought we'd look around in the stores first since Stephanie can't go shopping alone. Afterwards, we'll hit the bakery for lunch. I understand they have outside seating under an awning, so we're good even with any afternoon showers."

Wendy looked impressed. "You sure did your home-work. May I come? I haven't done anything like that for ages."

"Wish you could. You're welcome anytime," Stephanie answered .

Aaron agreed, trying to round us all up. "Okay troops. Time's a wasting. You're losing valuable shopping time, Stephanie. Let's boogey."

Once Aaron helped Stephanie into the chair, down the ramp we rolled. Our walk to the front gate was refreshing as a soft breeze blew in off the Gulf. I lifted my nose to smell the soft fragrance of the flowers, as well as the fresh-ness of the greenery. Of course, I sneezed.

By now, the gate attendant knew us, so he waved us through. Cool. I've never been past The Blue Cow on paws. We walked to the crosswalk in front of The Blue Cow and crossed the street. Then I saw it: The sign for Artisan's Village. Stephanie clapped her hands. I bet shopping for her was equivalent to running and playing tennis ball for me.

Each store had its own smaller sign on the main signpost. I looked straight ahead to see that the shops were lined up along a long wooden boardwalk. We had to go up a short ramp. Once at the entrance to the boardwalk, Aaron said, "Stephanie, look at all these shops. Where would you like to start?"

She gushed. "Oh, my goodness! I feel like a kid in a candy store. How about 'The Art of Jewelry' straight ahead."

Aaron appeared surprised to read the sign in their front window. "'Well behaved pets welcome.' That's great, Max. We don't have to wait outside. Let's go."

We went inside and I watched as Stephanie's eyes grew as large as my Frisbee as she looked in all the glass show-cases. A beautiful lady with long white hair and a heavy necklace of different colored glass beads came out from behind the counter to greet us.

"Welcome to The Art of Jewelry. My name is Zoe. Every-thing here is handcrafted by me or other island jewelers. If you'd like to look at any piece, please let me know. Most important, take your time to study all our inventory. As you can see, there's quite a bit squeezed into this small shop."

Zoe stopped talking to smile at me. She noticed my Two Turtles collar. "So, this is The Inn's famous Max." She stroked my back. "Would your little buddy like a home-made bacon cookie? I bake them at my condo for my dog Cliff using only veggie bacon. They're healthy and must be pretty tasty because Cliff just loves them."

I couldn't wag my tail fast enough. Veggie bacon, I never had any, but Nate has some for breakfast once in a while. She opened a big jar near her cash register and took one out. I could smell it from where I was standing. "Here you go, Max."

Aaron asked how she knew my name.

Zoe explained. "I know his name because Nate told us about Max right after he adopted him during one of our business owners' meeting. He's crazy about Max and showed us photos of Max's first days at The Inn. Nate said Max's photo will replace his own on his Innkeeper's business cards."

Wow! I'm even more famous than I thought. Anyway, as I lay down staying well behaved and chewing my cookie all the while hoping for another, Aaron and Stephanie looked around in all the cases.

Aaron spotted something he liked. "May I please see that necklace with the black silk chain?"

I watched Zoe unlock the case and take it out. It looked like some kind of shell and its iridescent surface almost hypnotized me.

Aaron admired the shell. "This shell's so shiny it throws off so many colors."

Zoe nodded. "You have a good eye for beauty as your choice in companions confirms. Each piece is unique. I design and make each one in my home studio. The spiral shell featured in this design is abalone. Some say wearing abalone brings inner peace, while encouraging you to speak your heart. I designed this pendant using the natural beauty of the shell. Its shape has not been altered just polished and protected with a clear coating. I braided the silk rope and made the shell's scalloped holder out of sterling silver. Before I retired and moved to Sanibel, I worked as a designer for one of the most prestigious jewelers in Chicago. I loved the art of designing so much I couldn't retire and not continue my art." She looked at Stephanie. "Would you like to try it on?"

Stephanie looked like I do when I drool at a treat. Time didn't matter to me since Zoe gave me another half of a cookie. As I continued to feast, Zoe, necklace in hand, walked around the back of Stephanie's wheelchair. "Please lift your hair for me."

Stephanie obliged.

Aaron watched and smiled as Zoe fastened it around Stephanie's neck and handed her a mirror. "That looks beautiful on you, Stephanie. I'll take it." He handed Zoe his credit card. Wow. He didn't even ask, "How much?"

Zoe looked at Stephanie. "Would you like to wear it or take it with you in a gift box?"

I watched Stephanie hold up Zoe's hand mirror again to admire the necklace.

Aaron laughed. "Thank you for asking. My guess is, from the look on her face, she'll wear it and. I'll take the gift box."

Stephanie seemed so excited, she sounded like she didn't know what to say. "Aaron, it's so lovely. I never expected this."

"I know you didn't, but I want to do this." He leaned over to kiss her cheek.

Zoe ran his credit card. "Thank you, Dr. Swift. I'll put the box with your receipt in the bag, along with another treat for Max."

I made out the best of all...two-and one-half cookies. Stephanie still held the shell in her hand. "It's so lovely. I love it. Thank you again, Aaron."

Aaron smiled. "It's as lovely as you are. It's like it was made for you. Think of this as a souvenir of our adventures together on Sanibel."

He kissed her other cheek. Wow. Must have been some date last night. Once we left Zoe's, Aaron asked, "What store would you like to visit next?"

"Maybe one more gift store because I'd like to find a

small gift for Wendy. She's been so kind to me. There's a fragrance store two doors down from here and it's on the way to the bakery."

"Well, what are we waiting for? Let's shop 'til we drop." Aaron laughed.

We walked by two stores before reaching "Island Fragrances." Well behaved pets were welcome here too. Nice. Just hope I don't start sneezing like I do when Nate puts on too much cologne. As soon as we entered, I immediately started to sneeze. So many strong scents coming at my extra sensitive doggy nose from all different directions at once, my snout was on overload.

Aaron looked at Stephanie. "Would it be all right if I leave you at the counter and take Max outside? Have someone come get me if you need anything or when you're ready to leave."

A short, slim woman in a black store uniform with her light-colored hair tied back with a hair clip walked over and responded to Aaron's request. "Don't worry, sir. My name is Ann and I'm the assistant store manager. I'll take good care of her."

Aaron nodded. "Nice to meet you, Ann." He reminded Stephanie as he took me outside. "Stephanie, I'll be on the bench right outside their front window. If you need me, just holler."

"I'll be fine," she replied. "My only dilemma will be that I'll have too many fragrances to test."

Aaron read his phone while I, grateful to be outside, watched Stephanie smell little white pieces of paper through the large store front window. Stephanie nodded to Ann, who was trying to assist her select a fragrance. She must have found the perfect one because she handed Ann a credit card. Ann wrapped two boxes in gift paper. Placing them in a gift bag with a receipt, she handed Stephanie her card before coming out to get us.

"We are all set," she said.

Aaron dashed me inside to fetch Stephanie and wheel her out onto the walkway. I made it in and out with only one good sneeze.

Stephanie beamed, holding the shell in one of her hands. "I bought Wendy some Frangipani fragrance and soap. It's such a sweet, soft fragrance. I hope she likes it. Oh, and Ann admired my gorgeous necklace."

Aaron smiled. "Stephanie, I'm sure Wendy will love your gift. I can smell it from here and it smells great."

I sneezed again.

"I think that's a sign that Max likes it, too. Okay now," he continued, "I don't know about you, but I'm starved. Off to the bakery we go."

The small French bakery was another two doors down from the fragrance store. Aaron led us to the bakery's small patio entrance. A young lady wearing a full apron over her uniform came outside to greet us. She had very short hair with one side just a bit longer than the other, bright eyes, and a smile that could charm a serial killer. Holding two menus, she looked down at me. "Hey Max, good to see you." She glanced at Aaron and Stephanie. "You must be staying at The Inn. It's such a beautiful place with such a beautiful dog."

That's me. She hugged me. I just loved that. "I'm Trix and I'll be your server. Let me show you to an outside table. I bet Max would like some ice water, especially if you walked here and have been shopping."

Stephanie nodded. "We sure have done both. I'm curious about how you know Max. It seems like everyone on this island knows him."

Trix petted me again. "Nate orders from our bakery for special events at The Inn. He drives over to pick his order up, with Max in the front seat. I help him load his trunk before giving this sweet boy a hug. Nate is so nice and gives me a tip for helping."

Stephanie chuckled. "Don't mind us. We're happy to be Max's human companions."

Trix showed us to a table under their huge awning. "I already have some menus for you. Dessert or light lunch?"

Aaron smiled. "We're going to be very bad today, so probably both."

Aaron helped Stephanie get up and sit on a patio chair. Once they were seated, Trix handed them menus. "We have a wonderful lunch special today. Three of our homemade mini croissants baked in house, filled with chicken, or egg salad, or tuna salad. If you want all three the same, we can do that. The plate comes with mixed greens in oil and vinegar."

Stephanie responded immediately. "Oh, that sounds perfect. I'll have the special with unsweetened iced tea."

Aaron ordered as well. "Since I'm a carnivore, I'd like mine with all chicken salad and a coffee. We'll decide on dessert after lunch. If you'll excuse me, I'm off to find the little boys' room."

Trix answered, "That's inside to the right of the counter. I'll be back with your drinks and something special for Mr. Max."

Aaron left us and I looked at all the outside diners. I recognized a few couples from The Inn.

Trix returned and interrupted my thoughts. "Here you are." She placed the drinks down and fished something out of her pocket. "Max, I know we're a people bakery, but Zoe supplies us with homemade doggy treats. She made these treats last night with apples."

Say no more, I'm in heaven.

Trix noticed Stephanie's necklace, "Oh, I see you've already met Zoe. Her work is so unique. That's such a lovely necklace, and it looks nice with your green and blue blouse."

Stephanie held it in her hand so Trix could take a closer look. "Thank you. Zoe does such intricate work. Aaron bought this for me before we came here."

Trix smiled. "That means he really likes you. That's what they say when your man buys you a special piece of jewelry. Zoe's beautiful jewelry is a little over my price range but one day I'll buy one. Here you go, Max."

Trix knelt to give me three paw-shaped mini biscuits. I could stay at this shopping center all day! She left just as Aaron returned. Right on time, someone from the kitchen brought out the lunch plates.

Stephanie's eyes lit up. "This looks perfect. Thank you."

Aaron didn't even take a peek. He just dug right in. A man after my own heart, I hoped he would drop some chicken salad. I'm not supposed to eat any, but I do love my chicken dog food.

Before he could take another bite, the cell phone in his shirt pocket lit up. He took it out and looked at the caller's number before he hurried to push his chair back. "Please excuse me. I have to take this." Aaron left for a quiet spot near the back of the patio to take the call. I watched his reaction. He looked upset. He turned around so his back was to us, I'm sure so we couldn't see his facial expressions. When he finished the call, he returned to the table.

CHAPTER
TWENTY-THREE

I watched as a look of concern crossed Stephanie's face. "Is everything all right?" she asked Aaron as he sat down.

He shrugged his shoulders. "I'll know more in an hour. Everybody's fine. That call concerned a work-related problem."

After his answer, their conversation became sparse and, at times, not at all. I think they both worried about what could happen because of that call. They finished their lunch, and I ate my cookies. We lingered at the little restaurant so long I fell asleep under the table listening to Stephanie and Aaron make nervous small talk. Suddenly, I woke up surprised when I heard their chairs move. Aaron helped Stephanie into her wheelchair and called me. "Okay, buddy. Wake up. We're heading back to The Inn."

I stood and shook myself, trying to loosen any mental cobwebs. We returned to The Inn at a snail's pace I'm sure so they could savor every moment together.

Stephanie broke the silence. "I can't wait to give Wendy the gift I bought her."

Aaron touched the top of her head. "I'm sure she'll love it. That was very thoughtful."

When we reached the front desk, Wendy was busy with Kate and Jeff. They smiled, looking happy to be together, a far cry from when they first met.

I overheard Wendy advise them. "Nate cleared Max for your dinner date tonight as well as the extra hour tomorrow for pizza. You may pick him up at seven because Max must have his dinner, water, and a brief rest."

Seven? Wow. Have I just become the first twenty-four-hour canine concierge? Kate turned and spotted me. "Look, there's our boy."

Kate and Jeff walked over and surrounded me with hugs. Kate winked, and said, "We'll see you in a little bit, sweetie."

They left and Aaron laughed. "Max, you're such a star. Everyone wants to spend time with you!"

Stephanie interrupted Aaron to talk with Wendy. "Wendy, I'd like to give you this small thank-you gift I bought in Artisan's village. Thank you for all the kindness you have shown both of us."

Stephanie handed her the small bag. Wendy removed the tissue paper to take out the two small boxes wrapped in floral paper. She opened them, surprised to find the bottle of frangipani fragrance and boxed soap. Excited, Wendy gave Stephanie a big hug before exclaiming, "I love them. Frangipani is my favorite. Thank you so much."

Stephanie replied, "We're the ones who should thank you. Oh, and Max has a couple of Zoe's cookies left over from lunch. I'll give them to you for safekeeping."

Aaron helped Stephanie out of the chair and rolled it behind the counter. Stephanie and Aaron soon disappeared into the elevator as Wendy brought me into Nate's office.

Nate hugged me and ruffled the fur around my neck. "Sorry buddy, no polishing your magic tricks or TV shows tonight. It looks like you've started another romance. Thanks to you, Kate and Jeff really like hanging out together. They asked earlier if you could join them on their date tonight. Hope you're not upset I said 'yes'."

I could never be mad at Nate. He's the doggy parent who rescued me and gave purpose to my life. I'll always be grateful. If there's any way I can help him, I will.

Nate kissed the tip of my snout. "Ready for dinner? Let's go up and get your favorite turkey dog food. Since I didn't have time to talk to them, I'll have to give them the ground rules before they take you with them."

Ground rules? How many more rules do I need? I have so many I could give some to the neighbors' dogs. Besides, how do I tell Nate, especially since I don't speak Human, that I've already had apple paw biscuits and veggie bacon cookies? But since dinner sounded extra good tonight, I decided to cooperate. We reached our apartment and Nate filled my bowls. I ate as much of my food as I could. Then I hit my water bowl like a speed boat. I was thirsty even after those two small bowls of water at the shopping center.

Finished! Whew didn't know I could squeeze that much food in. Nate brushed me, so I would look fab. I knew the date drill. He changed my bow tie into something more formal before he looked at his watch. "Ten to seven, we'll take a quick walk so as not to keep your fans waiting." He gave my matching leash a gentle tug; downstairs and outside we went before meeting up with Kate and Jeff right at seven.

Jeff and Kate were waiting by the front desk. Jeff held Kate's hand and smiled when Nate walked me over to them. "Hi. I want you to have a great time tonight, but I have rules for Max. As you already know, he's not to have any human food or drink. No staying out past the two hours approved. Please keep him as far back from the band's speakers as you can because a dog's hearing is much more sensitive than ours. Thank you in advance for doing this."

We were ready to leave when Aaron, looking distraught, stepped out of the elevator rolling a carry-on. I wished I could ask him what was wrong. As he approached the front desk, I nuzzled his leg, which brought a weak smile to his face. He petted my back before he leaned down to kiss the top of my head.

Aaron looked like he was about to cry. "Max, you are the most special dog I have ever known. I could never thank you enough for bringing Stephanie and I together. I'm sorry to have to say 'goodbye.'"

Looking at Nate, he said, "I received a phone call earlier this afternoon from my partner. His wife went into labor and needs emergency medical treatment. She's at the hospital and he will cover our patients until I can get home. As I always said, 'Babies can't wait.' I just broke the news to Stephanie about my predicament, and she's as sad as I am."

I watched our night manager, Josh's jaw drop as surprised as I was by this. Aaron continued, "Josh, please give me a print-out of my charges and put them on the card I left as a guarantee. I already asked the bellman to take my luggage to the front entrance and wait for my car."

Nate shook Aaron's hand as Aaron told him. "Nate, thanks again for making my visit so wonderful. Please thank Wendy when you see her tomorrow."

Josh interjected, "We're sorry you have to leave us earlier than expected. I'll take care of everything you requested."

Jeff wheeled Kate over to Aaron. "I'm so glad we met at the tennis center and when you return, we'll reschedule our tennis match."

Kate tried to hold back tears. "I met Stephanie one day by chance and we've had tea together several times. She's so kind and sweet. She told me she thinks the world of you."

Aaron leaned over to kiss her cheek. He told her, "I hope Stephanie and I stay in touch. She's the best thing that has happened to me in a very long time." His voice cracked. "Make sure you take care of this fine fellow here. I'm looking forward to that tennis match."

What? He pointed to Jeff. How about me? Kate was quick to answer. "I will, and we'll try to look after Stephanie as well." Aaron gave me one more pet before the bellman met him at the front door with his luggage. He waved and left to get his cat car. I couldn't help it. I was worried about Stephanie.

CHAPTER
TWENTY-FOUR

After Aaron's sudden departure, I noticed Kate staring out the front windows at his car driving away, looking sad. Jeff noticed her demeanor as well, because he reached for her hand.

Josh, trying to break the silence, attempted to change the mood to something more cheerful. "Okay, you two should get moving. You have two hours together with Max, and the clock has already started ticking."

Jeff rubbed Kate's shoulders. "Kate, what do you think about sending Stephanie a message to join us for coffee and breakfast tomorrow morning at eight-thirty?"

I saw a smile beam across Kate's face. "Jeff, that's a wonderful idea."

Josh, still standing next to us, overheard them. "I'd be happy to take care of that for you."

"Thank you. We'd appreciate that," Jeff responded before leading us to the front entrance. All the way to the tennis restaurant and tonight's Blues Club, I worried about Stephanie. She was so kind-hearted. I could tell by the way she looked at Aaron she really cared about him.

Our server gushed all over me. Kate and Jeff received some extra special treatment as well, probably because I accompanied them. After they enjoyed some great food, which I was lucky enough to taste after Kate accidently dropped a shrimp, and music they loved, we headed back to The Inn. The night clear and the air fresh, I sniffed the air. Oh, that night blooming jasmine and the sweet fragrance of frangipani delighted my nose but made me sneeze like crazy.

Kate heard me. "You're so cute even when you sneeze."

I smiled my best doggy smile. Surrounded by the darkness of night, I stopped, looked up, and barked. So many bright and shiny dots dazzled my eyes. Their sheer numbers and their clarity made tonight different from any other recent night sky. Jeff and Kate stopped their chatter to see what made me bark.

Jeff looked up in awe. "Wow. This sky is spectacular for a city boy. The stars are so dazzling and the sky so romantic. Max's bark gave us a heads up. I think he, along with the stars, are telling us that our future together will grow brighter and brighter each day."

I looked at Kate to see how she reacted. Tears streamed down her cheeks. I bet they were tears of joy brought on by the beauty of the night sky and Jeff's romantic thought.

He leaned down and kissed her cheek. He walked in front of her wheelchair and planted the most romantic kiss on her lips. Wow! My tail couldn't wag fast enough. Any faster and I'd topple over.

Kate interrupted their kiss and started to giggle, which made Jeff laugh. I looked over at her and she covered her mouth, trying to hide another giggle.

Jeff smiled. "Whoever thought by the way we met that

we'd end up like this. I bet Max was the only one who knew for sure."

I can't lie. I did have a strong hunch, but that last kiss exceeded even my wildest expectations.

Jeff glanced down in my direction and stroked my head. "Max, we love you. You're the reason for our happiness."

Kate wheeled herself closer and touched the top of my head, agreeing. "Max, you're the best thing that's happened to me besides Jeff." She took a quick peek at her watch. "Oh no! Where does the time go? We have to take Max back, otherwise Nate may not let him come with us tomorrow."

Say no more. Jeff grabbed my leash and got into position to push Kate's chair. I was ready to roll as the three of us raced back to The Inn. We ran up the ramp as fast as we could; any faster, we would have needed wings to fly into the lobby. Josh and Nate were waiting to greet us. They looked happy, although I sensed Nate looked relieved. For him to be at the front desk, we had to be late.

Jeff, trying to catch his breath from our race up the ramp, gave me a big hug and handed my leash to Nate. "Nate, we both appreciate the extra time with Max tonight more than you can imagine."

Nate, always the diplomat, smiled. "Glad to do it. I'm here because you were fifteen minutes late and I wanted to make sure you all got back okay. I know what great company Max is." He glanced down at me. "Ready for your walk, buddy?"

Wish I could answer in Human. By now, I was and ready to head home. It was a long day even for a young energetic pup like me. Before Nate and I reached the front door, we overheard Josh tell Jeff and Kate, "Stephanie received your invite to breakfast. She said eight-thirty would be terrific since she asked to take Aaron's morning time with Max. She added the coffee shop was perfect and that it would be her pleasure to treat you both."

Kate sighed. "That's nice of her but this will be our treat. I'm sure she's sad about Aaron's early departure. Having a couple of new friends to cheer her spirits would lift ours as well. Please send her a message that we'll be happy to meet her there."

We watched Kate and Jeff head to the elevator together, Nate and I walked down the steps for my last walk of the evening. Once back upstairs in my bed, knowing my day was done, I closed my eyes and was out like a light.

Nate shook me awake the next morning. I slept so soundly my eyes were still filled with sleep. I stretched my legs in the air and yawned.

As usual, Nate was more alert and ready to go than I was. "Okay buddy, your first appointment is at nine. It's 8:00, so we have time for water, a quick breakfast, and a short walk before you check in with Wendy."

Breakfast and a drink sounded real good to me. I watched Nate put some dry food in my dish before mixing it with my chopped roast beef dog food in a can. I wolfed down my breakfast and drank water like a camel filling up for desert duty before Nate took me for my very quick morning walk. "I hope Kate and Jeff can cheer up Stephanie."

Well, if they can't, I know I will. We went to the front desk where Wendy was waiting and anxiously tapping a pencil on the counter.

CHAPTER
TWENTY-FIVE

"Well, it's about time you two showed up. Nate, I received a message this morning from Bruce at The Florida Service Dog Training Center. Since it's Max's alma-mater and they are having a silent auction to raise money for the school, they wondered if you would donate a stay at The Inn."

He responded in seconds. "I'd be happy to donate a weekend stay at The Inn in honor of this fine young man. Our Max is the best dog ever. I'll go take care of that first thing." He patted the top of my head as Wendy handed him the message on his way into his office. Nate was the best pet dad ever. I wagged my tail before going directly to my concierge bed.

My 9:00 a.m. appointment turned out to be a local reporter named Sam from The Sanibel Island Weekly doing a feature story on the different jobs dogs have on the Island. He was a cheerful guy, middle-aged with dark hair, and a friendly smile and had the right personality for a reporter. He was so affable people opened up to him.

He shot Wendy one of his friendly smiles. "Hi, you must

be Wendy. I heard some great things about you from guests I met outside. If you can, I need some facts about Max verified, like where he was born, his age, and whatever special talents he has." Sam then rifled through his notebook. I'm sure to make sure he asked all the right questions. Once Wendy filled him in, he took a small camera from his pocket. "Would you please have Max stay on his concierge bed for his official job photo?"

After a few clicks, my work photos were finished. The three of us headed outside, where Wendy spotted two kids playing Frisbee. "Hi girls, would you like to have a photo with Max?"

Excited, one responded. "You bet we would."

Sam took out his cell phone to take notes to go along with the photos. "And what are your names and where are you from?"

The younger one answered. "My name is Rebecca, and this is my older sister, Alicia. We're from Jacksonville, Florida."

They sat on the top stair of the porch with me in the middle, smiled, and petted me for Sam's photo op. He thanked them. "I'll send Wendy copies of the photos so you can take them home with you. Thank you for posing. I have one more question. Have you attended Max's magic show?"

Thrilled, Alicia was happy to tell all she knew. "Max the Magnificent is amazing. He can tell a white cookie from a brown cookie without being able to see colors. He's a real magician. We loved it."

Sam jotted down more notes concerning his time with Alicia before questioning a few of our older guests sitting on the front porch about their walks with me. One named Pearl Stone relaxing on a rocker replied. "Walking Max is the best part of my vacation day. I only wish I could spend the entire day with him."

Sam, happy he had enough information, thanked Wendy. "This has been my most fun interview of the week, including the non-dog ones. Thank you for that." He tipped his baseball cap and left.

Finally, break time. I only had a few minutes until my time with Stephanie. At exactly ten, Stephanie stepped out of the coffee shop and into the lobby. Still using a cane, she appeared to be walking better. She shot Wendy a smile and said, "Max and I aren't going far. We're going to sit on that lovely front porch and look out at the wonderful view. I wish I could take Max home, but since I can't, I hope to spend as much time as possible with him before I go back to work."

I wagged my tail as I watched her pat her shorts pockets. I knew what that meant. Doggy treats! I can't wait. Of course, I tried to contain my excitement, but since I was a big puppy, I jumped around in circles.

Stephanie laughed. "Easy sweetie, these cookies are all yours. Let's go."

Wendy interrupted our love fest. "Stephanie, would you like me to walk Max out to the porch for you? When your hour's up, I'll return to take him inside."

Stephanie nodded, "Thank you. I appreciate your help since I'm still not that steady on my feet."

On our way out to the porch, Stephanie pointed to a straight back cushioned chair facing the Back Bay. Once seated, Wendy handed her my leash and went back inside. I stood near the arm of Stephanie's chair and licked her hand. I know I'm going to miss her after she leaves. For some reason, I've bonded with her more than any of the other guests I've ever met. Most humans would think it was about the cookies, but it's not that at all. I truly loved her. Stephanie touched the top of my head and I lay near her feet.

"Max," she began, "I know it's only been one day since Aaron left, but I miss him more than you can imagine. He texted me last night before bed and again this morning. He said he will do this every day until we can be together again. He's so sweet and thoughtful. That's why I fell in love with him so quickly."

Wow! Fell in love. I liked where this was going. Her voice dropped. His last text read, "I really miss you, but you can't text me back on this line. It's for work-related messages only. I am sending you another number to text me. I'm so tired I forgot about no personal messages on this line."

Stephanie then took half a cookie out of her pocket and gave it to me. "He added his other number before ending the text. Max, you and I will still have our hour in the morning, but I gave up our two-hour sessions in the afternoon since I can't walk you and another guest might like to see you. This afternoon, Kate and Jeff want to take you on a pizza date."

I really wouldn't mind just sitting here with Stephanie for two hours, but a pizza date sounded good too. Other guests who came by greeted us and asked about Aaron. I could see by the tears forming in Stephanie's eyes that those questions made it tough for her to deal with his absence. When our hour was up, Wendy popped out of the lobby to get me.

"See you tomorrow, Max." Stephanie kissed the top of my head before we went our separate ways.

CHAPTER
TWENTY-SIX

For the next two mornings, Stephanie and I sat in that very same spot on the porch at the very same time, but today our appointment was much later in the afternoon. I'm sure she changed her appointment to accommodate another guest who wanted to walk me. She liked to remind me, "You do know exercise like walking with guests is as good for you as it is for them."

Once I finished my last walk, I was ready for Stephanie, but for whatever reason, Stephanie was not her cheerful self today.

From her first words to me, I detected sadness in her voice. "Max, I heard from Aaron often the first two days after he left, but I've received no calls or messages at all so far today. I realize with his crazy work schedule, he communicates at different times. He tells me he's keeping track of me because I'm too good to lose. I never thought I'd fall in love again, let alone so quickly after my messy divorce, but you made all of this happen. Aaron mentioned in his very first text that he missed you and couldn't wait to see you again soon."

I sure hoped I see him again soon too, since that would mean Stephanie would as well. She reached into her pocket and gave me a biscuit. I don't know how she was able to get more cookies, but she did. Wonder if the doggy bakery delivered. I crunched my cookie just as the front door to The Inn opened and Kate wheeled herself out onto the porch. As soon as she saw us, she came over and parked her chair next to us.

I smiled and wagged my tail when I heard Kate tell me. "Max, you have the most irresistible smile!" She looked at Stephanie. "Hey girl, I know it's only been a few days, but how are you coping without Aaron?"

Stephanie shot her a forced smile, "I can't be any better at the moment. I'm with my best bud." She ruffled the fur around my neck. "Funny you should ask. I haven't heard from Aaron since yesterday. He hasn't answered my texts. I hope he's all right and just busy with work. Before he left, he said he'd like to arrange a long weekend for us at his home when he's not on call. I won't know how much time I can take off from work until I'm back in the saddle, but I'm sure we'll make that happen. Wish Max could come, but I don't think Nate will go along with that."

Kate studied Stephanie with kindness in her eyes. "I'm glad you're planning to meet again. I'm sure Jeff and I will face those same obstacles after we leave here." Giggling, Kate held up her left hand. She dangled her fingers in front of Stephanie's face. I barked, concerned Stephanie was in danger.

"Oh, Maxie." Kate laughed. "You are too cute. I'm not going to hurt her. I just wanted to show Stephanie this antique silver marquisate friendship ring Jeff gave me at breakfast this morning. He said it belonged to his grand-mother, and he wore it on a chain in her memory. Jeff took it off and placed it on my finger to show how committed he is to our relationship."

Wow! Jeff doesn't let any moss grow under his feet. I sniffed Kate's ring and put my chin on Stephanie's lap to get a closer look. It had a pretty oval setting and its tiny stones sparkled in the sunlight.

Stephanie held up Kate's hand to get a better look. "It's lovely and so is the old-fashioned way Jeff is committing. You are too young to remember, but my grandma showed me her friendship ring. She said your beau gives it to you before your engagement ring. Jeff sure didn't waste any time."

Kate smiled. "I'm in heaven. Jeff's grandmother told him to save it for that 'special young lady'. He said he knew I was the one. I can't believe something so beautiful is happening to me, especially after all the past putdowns, comments, and rudeness. I feel like I'm in a dream."

Being a dog was sometimes very difficult. Wish I could tell Kate she deserved to be this happy, and so does Jeff. Just then, Michael, The Inn's human concierge, carried out a round tray holding a pitcher of lemonade, two glasses, some human sugar cookies, along with my ice water in my doggy dish. He placed our goodies on the round wicker table between my two favorite ladies.

"Hi Stephanie and Kate, thought you might enjoy a cold drink. It's very warm out here." He filled their glasses and placed my water dish on the floor. Before he left, he reminded them. "If you need anything, just call the front desk."

Stephanie and Kate thanked Michael as I slurped my water. Boy, did I ever need that. It was hot today. As soon as he left, Stephanie started the conversation. "Never in my wildest dreams did I imagine I would meet anyone as special as Aaron, especially after my stressful divorce. I'm so happy and count the hours before I'll be with him again." As soon as she finished that statement, her cell buzzed. "What's this? Speak of the devil. It's a text from Aaron."

For some reason, I had an odd feeling and sensed the need to comfort her, so I placed my head under her arm. Stephanie read the text silently. I watched tears roll down her cheeks. When she finished reading, she sobbed. I tried to comfort her by licking her hand. I wondered what could be so wrong.

Kate took her hand. "Stephanie, is everything all right?'"

Still sobbing, Stephanie shook her head "no."

"Is there anything I can do to help?" Kate persisted.

Stephanie put her head in her hands and sobbed. "It's Aaron."

"Is he hurt or sick?" Kate continued.

Stephanie answered in between sobs. "He sent this awful e-mail to my cell."

She took a deep breath to compose her emotions before she continued. "He wrote, 'My dearest Stephanie, I hope after reading this you won't hate me. Beth has remained in contact with me since I arrived home. She reminded me that Stu left her and apologized for her past behavior. She asked for my forgiveness and wanted us to be a couple again. I didn't know what to do. I was torn—very torn. I knew how much I love you, but she recalled how great our life together had been until she messed it up, how we were to be married, and she was the reason we weren't. She asked for my forgiveness again before suggesting we meet in person to talk through "things." Once we met, I succumbed to her sadness and guilt about her treatment of me. I still don't understand why because she caused me a great deal of emotional pain. She then suggested I fell in love with you because both of us needed a romantic rebound and a new start. That's why she fell for Stu. Stu listened to her and showered her with attention.

'I'm sorry to tell you this through an e-mail, but I am renewing my relationship with Beth. Maybe she's right. Maybe we loved others on the rebound…you from Tyler, me from Beth. I think getting back with her is the right thing to do. She's in a great deal of heartache and I feel guilty about that. Thanks for all our wonderful times together. With love and my deepest respect, Aaron.'"

"The right thing to do?" Stephanie asked, bewildered. "Thanks for the wonderful times. Has this guy lost his mind?"

Once again, I wish I could talk Human to console Stephanie and talk sense into Aaron. I'm sure he didn't fall back in love with Beth. That was his soft touch and physician's empathy caving into Beth's wishes and did not express the true feelings in his heart.

I looked over at Kate, whose mouth was wide open and remained speechless. She kept squeezing Stephanie's hand until she said. "Surely you should call him. He's not thinking straight. I've seen the look of love in his eyes whenever he looked at you and the joy in his heart that gave him that bounce in his step."

Stephanie shook her head. "No. I can't talk to him now. The pain in my heart stabs too deep."

Kate would not let up. "Then let me talk to that man."

Another "no" from Stephanie; I wanted to step in, but what could I do?

Stephanie, still crying, got up, took her cane, and left for her room. She passed a concerned Wendy at the front desk.

I followed Stephanie as close as I could with my leash dangling behind me. I needed to make sure she was all right. Stephanie tried to wipe her tears with her hand before glancing down at me. She blew me a kiss and stepped into the elevator. I stood by the door, watching it close as Kate wheeled herself into the lobby and to Wendy.

When I saw Kate, I walked back to the front desk.

"Wendy, did Stephanie tell you about Aaron's e-mail ?"

"No, is everything all right?"

Kate paused. "No. Far from it. I don't think Aaron's in his right mind. He broke up with her by e-mail. What kind of heartless person does that? I've met Aaron and can assure you he's not heartless or uncaring. On the contrary, he's empathetic and sympathetic. Bet his callous ex, must have tugged on those qualities because he wrote that he decided to go back to her. You remember she's that selfish woman who cheated on him and canceled their wedding."

I observed the surprised look on Wendy's face. "But why? He's crazy about Stephanie."

"I don't know. I guess Beth appealed to his soft heart and guilt. We must do something. I'm sure Aaron loves Stephanie, and she loves him."

"But what can we do? They're hundreds of miles apart and even worse, not talking," Wendy responded.

Kate shrugged and left for her room, looking very concerned. I dug deep into my service dog training instincts. What would bring Aaron here and keep Stephanie from going home alone? What did they share in common while they were here?

I lay by Wendy's feet with my head in my paws. She stroked my neck and reflected. "It's sad. They make such a wonderful couple. I wish I could help them reconcile, especially since they both love you so very much, Max. Perhaps

I should ask Nate what to do. I'll go into his office and get his advice."

After she said that, my head popped up like a jack in the box. That's it! What Wendy said was it! She's a human service dog who guided me to the right answer. What did Aaron and Stephanie have in common? It's their love for me, so what can I do to get them together? Think, Max, think!

As soon as Wendy left to see Nate, my mental wheels spun like a top. My ears perked up when I heard the elevator doors open. I watched Stephanie using her cane step out and head to the front desk. She glanced at me with tearful red eyes and knelt by the counter, hoping I'd go see her. "Max, please come here, sweetie. I need some of your furry love in a big way now more than ever. Sorry, I left you so abruptly. I needed to be alone or so I thought, but I realized when I'm down, you're my best pick me up medicine."

I got up and walked slowly to where she knelt. I wagged my tail weakly when, as I did, a light bulb went off in my head. That's right. She said it herself; I was her best medicine. What would happen if she had no best medicine? That's when I decided to put my plan into action, and I wobbled a bit before collapsing on the floor near her feet. I stretched my tongue out and breathed deep and slow.

Stephanie looked down at me and frantically called, "Max? Max, are you all right?" I didn't move nor did I acknowledge her call in any way. She gently shook me, trying to get a reaction. Still unable to obtain one, Stephanie, beside herself, pounded the service bell on the front desk counter seeking assistance. "Help! Help! Something's wrong with Max! Please come. Max has passed out and I can't get him to respond. Nate, Wendy, anyone please come to the front desk now to help us. It's urgent."

"Max?" Wendy and Nate responded in echo as they opened the door to Nate's office. They couldn't run fast enough to where we were.

Stephanie cried out, "Look at how lifeless he is. I'm sure he doesn't even know I'm here."

Nate, I'm sure beside himself with worry, came running over to me first. He held my head in his hands. "Max, please, open your eyes. Look at me, buddy. I love you so much. You know I'm here for you."

When I kept my eyes closed and didn't look at him, he gently raised my eyelids. "Wendy, please call Dr. Rose. Tell her Max is very sick and unconscious. Tell her it's an emergency."

I squinted to watch Nate take a piece of paper out of his wallet and hand it to Wendy. "She wrote her private cell number for me on the back of her card. Tell her it's urgent. Her office is off island. I only hope she can get here in time. Find Matt and ask him to come help me move Max into my office, so he'll be more comfortable. Tell Matt to bring a blanket."

A blanket in 80-degree heat? With my furry coat? That's quite a novel approach to wellness. I heard Wendy run on the tile floor to the phone on the front desk. She called Dr. Rose's private cell and held the phone away from her ear so we all could hear the doctor's recorded message. Crying into the phone, Wendy pleaded. "Please come at once to The Inn, Dr. Rose. Max is not responding to anything. He collapsed, trying to greet one of our guests. This is an emergency. Please help!"

The doctor interrupted the recording and answered. Wendy placed the phone on speaker so we could all hear Dr. Rose's response. "Max? Collapsed? Say no more. I'll be right there."

I heard Nate breathed a deep sigh of relief after Dr. Rose's reply. Matt who by now came to the lobby, helped Nate carry me into his office and onto the soft area rug in front of Nate's desk. Wendy and Stephanie followed.

Stephanie was still crying. "We need to do something. We have to help him. I love him so very much."

Squinting, I saw Wendy squeezing Stephanie's arm, saying. "We all do."

My body remained as still as a statue, while I kept my legs limp in case someone tried to lift one. Nate, anxious to have me come to, tried to get my attention by waving my favorite peanut butter cookie under my nose. I couldn't try to sniff it because I had to keep my head down and my eyes closed. Hardest thing I had to do so far to make this charade work.

I heard voices in the front lobby. One sounded like Dr. Rose's. Wow, she must have broken the sound barrier to get here this fast. I've heard from other dog owners in her waiting room that her name suits her. Whenever she laughs, her entire face blushes a deep rose. Matt escorted Dr. Rose into Nate's office. I peeked through a slit in one eye. She wore a flowered sundress, not her usual animal print scrubs and had pearls instead of a stethoscope around her neck.

Dr. Rose explained her speedy appearance to Nate. "I was right off the property having lunch with an old friend at the bakery across the street when I received Wendy's call. That's how I could get here so quickly."

Hmmm. Wonder if she brought me any cookies from Zoe's? In a reassuring voice, Dr. Rose took charge immediately. "Please, everyone except for Nate, leave the room. Don't worry. I'm going to take good care of Max, but he doesn't need any extra stress at the moment."

From the corner of my mostly closed eye, I could make out Wendy blowing me a kiss from the door to Nate's office. Stephanie, reluctant to leave me, still sobbed. "Someone should let Aaron know about Max. I refuse to talk to that man after he broke up with me by e-mail this morning. I guess you could say my day has gone from bad to worse, but I do know he loves Max as much as I do."

Wendy hugged Stephanie. "I'm so sorry about what happened this morning. Don't worry. I'll call Aaron and let him know. The doctor in him will want to examine Max personally. Anyway, we should leave so Dr. Rose can treat Max."

Keep that thought about Aaron in mind, Wendy. Hope Aaron becomes so worried he must come right away to see me. Once it was just us three in Nate's office, Dr. Rose opened her bag of tricks. She checked my heart and listened to my breathing.

"Huh. You said or Wendy did that this happened suddenly. He was about to greet a guest and just collapsed. Who was the guest?"

Nate nodded. "He was with Stephanie Jakes when he collapsed. I tried to give him his favorite cookie, but he refused it like it wasn't even there. That's not at all like him. Please tell me. How sick is he? Could it be food poisoning, or could he have eaten a poisonous plant? Do you need to take him to the clinic for bloodwork? How can I help?"

Dr. Rose looked down at me and shot me a motherly smile. "No, no, and no. I believe he's fine and that this attack might be psychosomatic. His strong heartbeat, and strong lungs, not to mention his body temperature, lead me to that conclusion."

Careful not to open my eyes more than a crack, I glanced up at Nate.

"Psychosomatic?" he asked. "Dogs can have episodes like that?"

"Sure," my good doctor said with ease. "Police dogs and military dogs have this happen frequently. Let me ask you. Was Max close emotionally to Stephanie and did she have a stressful issue he could sense?"

"Max is very close to her and to Aaron whom she's been dating. They have become very close in such a short time. That's why it was a surprise when Aaron broke up with her by e-mail. Wendy said Max was with Stephanie when she received that email from Aaron breaking up with her this morning. Do you think Max is capable of understanding what happened?"

"I'm not sure about that, but by Stephanie's reactions, he sensed something bad happened to her. From my limited exam, I'm happy to report that I believe your little stinker here is a big faker."

Darn, why does she have to be so smart? My way too smart vet continued. "What could be gained by his behavior?"

"Well, Aaron left us a few days ago. He broke up with Stephanie this morning. Wendy and I discussed what would bring Aaron back to The Inn to face Stephanie and make him realize what a big mistake he made. We were about to call him, but that was right before Max collapsed."

"What kind of mistake?" Dr. Rose asked.

"Aaron decided to get back together with his former fiancée, Beth, who had cheated on him with his best man and called off their wedding with no warning. Before Aaron left, we all could see how he looked at Stephanie and sensed how much he cared about her. In recent days, Beth convinced him that he fell for Stephanie on the rebound." Nate petted me again. "Are you sure Max is really okay?"

The doctor nodded. "I'm positive he is. Do you think Aaron would return to The Inn if he knew Max was very sick?"

Nate puzzled. "I'm sure he would. So, you're telling me that this little stinker is trying to bring them back together?"

Dr. Rose said, "Again, I'm not sure if he's quite that smart. I think this act or response may be a reaction to Stephanie's sadness."

I sure am that smart. Since my gig was up, I picked up the cookie Nate left under my nose and crunched it.

"There you see." Dr. Rose said, pointing to me. "Caught in the act!"

I wagged my tail not knowing how much trouble I was in, so I stood up and shook.

"Why that little actor seems fine," Nate responded. "I don't know whether to scold him or hug him, but he may just have found the answer to our dilemma. If he pretends to be so sick that Aaron decides to come back to see him, Aaron and Stephanie might have a chance meeting and renew their relationship. Doctor, would you help us pull this off. Of course, I'll pay for your time. Please tell everyone that Max is sick. Very sick. This will remain our secret. Max, can you play dead?"

I smiled and wagged my tail. Of course, I could, but wondered if these two humans could keep my secret with a straight face.

Dr. Rose covered her mouth to hide her laughter before she took out two bottles of large pills from her case. "I'm in. Let's get started. These are both chewable vitamins. They're just different sizes and colors. They must taste good because my other patients gobble them up. I'll take the labels off the bottles and replace them with hand-written ones that sound like prescription drugs. I'll handle the diagnosis and inform your staff."

Nate filled my water dish from his own bottled water. I drank as Nate pointed his finger at me. "Max, if you can hang in there and keep this act up, we might get a visit from Aaron."

Hang in there? Remember, I was the one who started this fake illness. I was one of the most talented at learning commands in service dog school, even though I didn't like to follow them. Nate doesn't realize it, but he's talking to a real pro. I wagged my tail to let him know I was one hundred percent ready to do this.

Dr. Rose chuckled at my eagerness. She ruffled the fur on my head. "Okay, my sweet boy, give this everything you've got."

Nate gave me another cookie before telling me to, "Lie down. Play dead."

I assumed the same position as I did in the lobby. Nate put another cookie under my nose. UGH. That was torture, but I was ready to help Stephanie and Aaron reunite any way I could while anxious to see how Dr. Rose would help me make this happen. She looked at us.

"You two stay here. Max, stay in that same position. Nate, put the two bottles of pills on your desk and pull on your hair like you're really stressed. I can't lie. This is the most fun I've had in years. I'll go out to the front desk and tell your troops our story."

With that, she turned and went out to the front desk, closing the office door behind her, but leaving it open just a crack so we could hear what she said and how the others responded.

CHAPTER
TWENTY-SEVEN

As soon as Dr. Rose stepped into the lobby, I heard gasps followed by "How is he?" and "Will he be all right?'

Wendy spoke first. "I reached Aaron. He was so devastated by Max's sudden illness. He's on his way here as we speak to see if he could be of any help. He said lucky for him, his partner is back in the office, so he was able to leave. I'll let everyone know when he arrives. Please, Dr. Rose, may we see Max?"

Stephanie listened. "Thanks, Wendy, for doing that. I hope Aaron can help Max, but I do not want to see him now or ever."

Dr. Rose paused in good doctor style. As soon as Wendy and Stephanie finished, I heard my vet take a deep breath, probably trying to control another one of her spontaneous chuckles. "I have good news and some bad. The good news is I think Max will survive, but his recovery will take time. I think his symptoms lead me to believe he ingested a plant that is known to have a bad reaction in dogs, one that in large quantities can be poisonous. I advised Nate to let him rest and since it's not a good idea for him to walk or exert himself as of yet, I've ordered some doggy diapers for him from my clinic."

"What is the name of the plant?" Stephanie asked, concerned. "I hope that didn't happen when he was with me. I'd never forgive myself."

Dr. Rose, I'm proud to say, was quick on her feet. "Without proper testing, I'm not one hundred percent sure until we get the lab results. I'm taking a blood and urine sample with me when I leave. I did notice oleander growing next to the front porch. Oleander can be lethal to dogs. If that's what he ingested, he must not have eaten very much; just enough to make him sick, but not kill him."

All I could hear was "Oh my gosh." and "Those bushes must go." The last statement sounded like it came from Wendy.

I heard Dr. Rose clear her throat to get everyone's attention again. "Ahem. I gave Max a pill to make him throw up and some antibiotics to take after he does. That first pill acts pretty fast, so I'd give him some space to make all this happen."

Nate made pretend throw up noises before he covered his mouth, trying not to laugh.

More concern from Wendy and Stephanie, who continued to ask in unison, "May we please see him? We're so worried."

My savvy vet interrupted them. "Nate will advise you when Max can have visitors. Max will more than likely go to sleep after throwing up whatever he can of the poison. I know how concerned you both are, but please don't disturb them. I'll come back tomorrow and check on him. I told Nate to call me at any hour if there are any changes to Max's condition before I return."

Wow. Dr. Rose killed it! That was an Academy Award worthy performance. As soon as she finished, I heard Wendy and Stephanie thank her.

Wendy added, "Dr. Rose, I'm sure we would have lost Max without your quick response. When you're ready to leave, may I see you to your car? I'll let Matt know to bring your car around to the front entrance."

Dr. Rose, handing Wendy her keys, replied, "Thank you, but first I must make one last check on Max."

She came back into the office, closed the door, and picked up her medical bag. "Aaron's on his way. You two stay on message and we may bring our two lovebirds back together."

I heard the doctor's car stop near the front entrance and Wendy chat with Dr. Rose before she left.

Stephanie stayed outside of Nate's office and sobbed. Wish I didn't have to be so sneaky. It's not in my nature, but it's for Stephanie and Aaron's own good. Once we heard Wendy return, Nate signaled for me to stay in my sick position and got up to go to the lobby to comfort Wendy and Stephanie. He left the door ajar a bit wider because their voices came through clearer than before.

I heard Wendy ask first. "Oh Nate, I'm so heartbroken. I love that little guy. How's Max doing?"

Nate paused for effect. "Wendy, the doc's happy. At the very least, he's holding his own. She said it could take up to seventy-two hours for him to pass this crisis. I'm going to get washed and will come back to sleep on the couch in my office. He'll be all right until I return."

"How can we help?" Wendy asked.

Nate responded, "Please get me some sheets and a light blanket and pillow from the supply closet. I'd appreciate it."

Stephanie asked, "Can I get you something to eat?"

"No. I'm too nervous and worried about Max to eat. I'll be right back. I need some clean clothes from the residence. Please leave him alone to rest."

With that, I heard Nate close the door and lock it. At last, I get some relief from playing dead. I quietly stretched and stood for a few minutes. I assumed the sick position when I heard Nate's key in the lock and chatter by the office door. Whew! I lay down just in time. Nate opened the door a crack.

I could hear Stephanie crying. "I love Max so much. Aaron called my cell to check on him but since I don't want to talk to that man, I let the call go to voice mail. His message said he's less than an hour away and wants Nate to know even though he's a human doctor, he'll help Max in any way he can."

Nate sighed. "I appreciate that."

Wendy returned. "May I help you set up this bedding? Oh, the vet sent over Max's diapers with her assistant. I have them at the front desk and will leave them by the door."

Nate responded, "Thanks for your help. I appreciate it since I may not get much sleep tonight. Let me put this bedding in my office and I'll come back out for the diapers. I know you both want to be with him, but remember Doc Rose said no visitors."

Nate unlocked the door. I remained in my sick pose as he went back out for the diapers. He went back inside the office, closed, and locked the door. He whispered, "Good boy. I'll keep the office door locked tonight so you can stretch out and we can get some sleep."

What's this? He pulled two small plastic bags from his pants' pocket. One had mini cookies and a teeny amount of my dog food. The other smelled like a peanut butter and jelly sandwich. How great was that? Nate opened his door a crack to make sure everybody had left. They did, so we relaxed.

About an hour later, I heard a car pull into our circular driveway. It was twilight, so the approaching headlights shone through the cracks in office's wooden shades. I'd bet a doggy cannoli, it was Aaron's cat car.

The car stopped. We soon heard a car door slam and Aaron's voice. "Please help me with my bag."

Great! Aaron's here! I heard footsteps on the tile floor in the reception area. Wendy and Stephanie must have heard his car as well, because they returned to the lobby.

I heard Wendy's voice. "Aaron, we're all so happy you came. Max may need your help."

"Where is he now?"

"He's on medication and in Nate's office not to be disturbed."

Aaron sounded disappointed. "But I hoped to examine him tonight."

Stephanie remained quiet as Wendy responded. "Nate knows and appreciates that, but Max's vet said no visitors tonight. How are you? You look so pale and tired. Have you eaten today?"

That's my Wendy. Mother to all.

Aaron replied. "My partner came back to work today. I've been on call for twenty-four hours straight before you phoned about Max. My entire system is out of sorts. I guess I could use something to eat."

Wendy replied, "Good. A strong cup of coffee and some nourishment will help you think better. Let's all go to the coffee shop. It's open late."

I heard Stephanie angrily say, "Not on your life will I go

anywhere with that man. Wendy, you can let go of my arm."

I always knew my Wendy was as persistent as a beaver building a dam but wondered if her plea would work. She told Stephanie. "Look, we should put our personal feelings aside to help Max. He may need Aaron's assistance. Please come with us."

Aaron added to Wendy's plea. "Stephanie, I don't blame you for not wanting to spend one minute with me after I e-mailed you. Let's put Max's health first and afterwards, maybe we could talk."

"Okay, I'll go, but I have nothing to talk to you about Aaron unless it concerns my Max."

I didn't hear any more conversation, so I guessed they left for the coffee shop. I hoped Wendy, through her kind nature, would get them to talk and something good would come of their meeting. Once I no longer heard them, I sat up and ate some dog food from a spare dish Nate kept in the cabinet behind his desk along with two more cookies.

Nate enjoyed his sandwich with a diet soda from his small office fridge while reading his hotel association magazines. I'm guessing it was a little more than an hour before they returned. I heard a faint knock on the door.

Nate got up, put my dish out of sight, and signaled for me to play dead, as he opened the door a crack. "Aaron, thank you for coming. I can't express how much I value your concern and support. The little guy is family to me."

Aaron paused. "We all love him. If you'd let me, I'd like to examine Max. You know how much I care about him and even though I'm a doctor for humans, I might be able to help."

Oh, no. Aaron's too smart. He'll know what I'm up to. Thank goodness Nate was as smart as a whip, maybe even savvier than the good doctor. "I really appreciate your help but his vet Dr. Rose gave him a mild sedative, and he's sound asleep. She said he's not to be disturbed because sleep will help him get better and stronger. I'd love for you to look at him, but let's do it tomorrow morning. Do you have a place to stay? You've only been gone a few days, and I held your reservation for the bridal suite in case you decided to return before your scheduled time here was up."

"Thank you. That's very kind. Wendy is here along with Stephanie, so maybe she can check me in again. We all just returned from the coffee shop. You stay with my boy, Max, and I will check on him in the morning. If you need me in the middle of the night, please call me…"

From the corner of my eye, I could see Nate stick his hand out for Aaron to shake. "Good night to you and Stephanie, and of course, Wendy." With that, Nate closed the office door.

"To you and Stephanie." I just loved the sound of that. We waited a few minutes.

Nate peeked out to make sure Aaron had left before he gave me the thumbs up that it was okay for me to walk around. He chuckled. "I don't know how much longer we can keep this charade going. I hope they have a chance to talk and make up soon."

It was late. I lay down again snuggled on that soft throw with Nate stretched out on the couch. We fell asleep. That night I had the most wonderful dream about Stephanie and Aaron kissing in a field of wildflowers.

CHAPTER
TWENTY-EIGHT

B right sunlight broke through the slats of the wooden window shades and woke me. I needed to go out but that might prove difficult.

Nate stopped snoring suddenly and opened his eyes. "You okay, Max. Need to go out?"

Did I ever? His statement was music to my ears. I panted and wagged my tail like crazy. Nate went into the adjoining bathroom and brought back a bath towel. "Dr. Rose said, using this when you walk will make your weakness look real. She said it's done after certain surgeries and major illnesses. I'll try not to hurt you in the process."

I should hope not. I stood and he placed the towel under and across my tummy. He then lifted the towel at both ends before we went outside through the office door. I wiggled because this towel thing was very uncomfortable. He coaxed me. "Easy, Max easy."

Our timing couldn't have been worse. As soon as we walked out the office door, I saw Wendy getting out of her car, ready for work. It must be 7:00 a.m. I pretended to struggle to lift my leg and do my business. She spotted me and called out. "Max! Max, you're up. How wonderful!"

Yikes! Wonderful for her. I'm not supposed to be energetic, so I tried as hard as I could to look weak and tired. Nate waved. "Wendy, as you can see, Max got through the night okay. He did have to use the diapers which I have bagged and disposed of in the dumpster. We're going back into my office for more rest. If you need me to help with anything, please call my cell."

Wendy nodded and tried to follow us, but we made it inside the office before she could reach us. Nate locked the outside glass doors and pulled the drapes. Wendy stopped short and turned because she now had to use the front entrance. She knocked to let us know she was at her post.

Nate opened the office door a crack and held out my water dish. "Wendy, please fill this with spring water for Max. I need to stay with him."

She took my dish but as she turned to leave, I heard the elevator doors open and her say, "Stephanie and Aaron, how nice to see you together. Aaron, is Stephanie all right? I see you have your arm around her waist, helping her walk."

Nate left his door open a crack.

Stephanie groaned like she was in pain. "No, I'm far from it. I slammed the side of my leg against the bed frame, trying to get back into bed last night in the dark. Anyway, I always keep my cell on me at all times but didn't think about using the light. I didn't want to bother Nate with Max sick and all, so reluctantly I called Aaron. He was nice and did come right away to help me up and examine my leg. He said my leg was probably badly bruised and offered to take me to get it checked since there was swelling and the bruise was turning colors, but only after he examined

Max. He then made me an ice pack and brought me an Ibuprofen to reduce any swelling. I offered to pay him for his medical services, but he refused my offer, saying all he wanted was a chance to talk to me about everything that happened between us. So, because of his care, I agreed to have coffee with him after my doctor's exam and listen, but listening is all I agreed to do. That's not as important as my next question. How's Max?"

Wendy's voice reflected her enthusiasm from today's events so far. "That was so nice of Aaron to help you, considering how tired he was. I hope he's right, and you did only suffer a bruise. When I arrived this morning, I saw Max outside with Nate. Nate had to hold him up with a towel, but even so how wonderful is that?"

Nate then stepped out of his office to give them an update on my condition. "Max is better this morning. I took him outside as Wendy already told you, helping him balance with a towel."

"That is so wonderful," Stephanie exclaimed.

Nate responded. "Yes. I'm so relieved. Stephanie I'm sorry to hear you fell. If there is any way I can help, please let me know."

Stephanie gushed "I don't care about my bruises, only that Max is better. That's the best news I could ever hear today. Thanks for your encouragement. Aaron called and asked to examine my leg again this morning. He called from my room and made an appointment for me to check-in with the specialist who diagnosed my fracture to see how it's healing, especially since my bruises are on that same leg. He's located in the medical building next to the hospital. We're on our way there after Aaron checks on Max."

Aaron picked up on her last statement right away. "May I examine Max now?"

Oh, boy. How will Nate ever get out of this one? I know he's quick on his feet, but Aaron is so persistent and I'm sure will not give up.

"Sure but let me give him a light breakfast while you take Stephanie to visit the doctor. Max is alert and able to get up and down with my assistance, so don't rush. Stop for breakfast or coffee on your way home. As soon as you return, he's all yours."

Aaron sounded happy to hear that. "That's great! He appears to be on the mend. I'll check him when we get back. Ready to see Dr. Sawyer, Stephanie? I'll go get the car."

"Ready."

Nate kept the door open while they left. I continued to play weak but could now keep my eyes open. Nate was always prepared. Besides a spare dish, he kept a secret stash of dogfood packets in his cabinet in case of an emergency. I haven't quite figured out what constituted a dog food emergency but was glad he did.

Wendy returned with my water bowl, Nate took it, and closed the door. He then rinsed my food dish in his small restroom and emptied two packets of food into it. I ate like a champ but stopped when we heard Wendy knock. "Nate, can I get you anything? Coffee? Breakfast?

Nate responded, "I could sure use some coffee. By the way, how are Stephanie and Aaron getting along? They at the very least appeared civil this morning. I hope they have a chance to talk things out."

Wendy laughed. "Can't say for sure, but they're not at each other's throats. When Aaron left to get his car, Stephanie said that when Aaron came to help her last night, their mutual concern for Max's well-being provided a chance to start a conversation between them. She said their mutual worry made them realize what was really important in their lives."

Nate sounded encouraged. "They seem like they were made for each other. I sincerely hope they can work things out."

No more than me. I love both of them. Later that morning, I heard the front door buzzer.

Someone was here. I heard a familiar voice say. "Hello, anyone home? It's Dr. Rose."

Wendy greeted her. "Good morning, Doctor. Max seems better this morning. Please follow me." I heard the two women approach the office.

Nate opened the door wide enough to let my vet enter. Once the door closed, Dr. Rose whispered to him. "Max must act better today. Considering that small amount of plant poison he supposedly ingested, the medicine should make him begin to turn around in twenty-four hours. By now, he should just be exhausted but able to get up today and walk slowly."

"You mean like a service dog?" Nate asked.

"Slower," Doc Rose answered as she looked at me. "You can get up now, Max. Okay? Stand."

You can't imagine how happy I was to hear those words, especially the last one. Once up, I shook myself and wagged my tail. She had Nate practice walk me as slow as a turtle around the room. Slow was an understatement. Any slower and I'd fall asleep standing up.

"That a boy! You're doing great, Max." Nate encouraged me. "Now, let's take our show out to the lobby."

By the joyful look on Wendy's face when I stepped into the lobby with Nate, someone would think she won the lottery. Dr. Rose followed us. Surprised beyond belief, Wendy rushed over to give me a hug. My head in her arms,

I saw the front doors open as Stephanie and Aaron stepped inside, and what's this? They're smiling.

"Aaron and I shared nothing but wonderful events today." After seeing me, she gushed. "Well, this makes three! Max, I'm so happy to see you!" Stephanie came over to hug me. "Max is up. My fracture is on the mend. My sprain is better, and those bruises will heal. And there's more, Aaron and I reconciled over breakfast. He apologized for sending me that heartbreaking e-mail. He told me with tears in his eyes that seeing me in person made him realize how wrong he was to treat me like that. What a great day!"

Aaron cleared his throat. "I guess I felt obligated to get back with Beth since my workaholic behavior made her look to Stu for attention and caused our split. Beth kept pushing for me to come back to her, even though that was the last thing I wanted. I never wanted to get back together with her romantically. I just wanted us to become friends. Beth wouldn't accept my offer of friendship and kept repeating that my feelings for Stephanie were on the rebound."

Wendy stepped aside so Aaron could be by my side. He held my face and looked into my eyes. "Max, I can't tell you how happy I am that you're better. You can't imagine what a scare you gave all of us. I'm still going to give you a thorough exam later."

He was persistent, but I was afraid of that. He stroked my back and kissed the top of my head. Kneeling by my side, Aaron looked up at everyone. "Sending Stephanie that e-mail was the dumbest thing I ever did. You all know how much I love her. After I arrived home, Beth texted me that she wanted to 'talk'. I was courteous and met with her. She said she was sorry she left me and hoped we would get back together. She could arrange another fancy wedding for us in less than two months. I felt sorry for her. Imagine that? After all she did to hurt me behind my back, I'm the one who felt sorry for her. And the biggest thing on her mind was not my feelings, but a fancy wedding. I think I carried my compassion a bit too far."

Stephanie interjected. "That's why I love you. You have a big heart and sometimes care about others more than yourself."

Aaron chuckled. "Maybe a bit too much. I told Beth we could become friends, but she wouldn't have it. She said after Stu left and after losing me, she fell into a deep depression and considered causing harm to herself."

Aaron sighed. "Beth ordered me to send that awful e-mail to Stephanie, or she assured me I would be sorry if I didn't. I would never see her again. I guess I either wasn't strong enough to say' no' or didn't want to know what she meant by sorry, especially after her threat. At that moment, I didn't think. As a doctor and someone who cared for her as a friend, I was trying to do everything in my power to prevent Beth from hurting herself or perhaps doing something worse. Since Beth doesn't know I'm here, I'll arrange to meet her at a location convenient for the three of us once Stephanie and I return home. If she tells us she's considering causing harm to herself again, I'll inform her parents about her depression and advise them to seek professional help for her."

Everyone remained quiet until Nate broke the silence. "You two have been through so much in such a short time. I hope things continue to get better for you."

"As long as we're together and Max is on the mend, we'll be fine. After all, Max is the reason we met and has brought us back together, although out of worry for him." Aaron responded. "Since I still have vacation time left and

Stephanie received an okay to extend hers, we plan to stay until Max is back to normal. Only good things are in store for us going forward."

Nate walked me slowly to the front entrance so I could go outside and take care of my business. Wendy, Stephanie, Aaron, and Dr. Rose applauded as I walked down the front steps. All the way down, I hoped Stephanie and Aaron would stay together for a long time.

CHAPTER
TWENTY-NINE
THREE MONTHS LATER

N ate adjusted my bow tie one more time. It was fancier than the usual ones I wear for weddings. He said, "I want you to look better than perfect if that's even possible since I think you're perfect the way you are."

Nate continued to readjust my tie for the sixth time. "The bride chose this lavender floral design to match the color of her attendants' gowns."

I've appeared in quite a few weddings since I arrived here, but usually know ahead of time who's getting married. I guess Nate must have rented me out for this one, probably to pay for my extra fancy dog food and gourmet treats.

"Maxie, I want you to look amazing. You've done this so many times before, but you'll soon see why this wedding is so special." Nate, wearing a dark suit and a tie that matched my bow tie, fastened my matching leash, and walked me downstairs to the lobby. Wow! Even Wendy had dolled up for this event; her hair curled, her make-up perfect, she wore a long crepe gown with sequins and looked amazing. By the look in Nate's eyes, I think he thought so, too.

She took one long look at us and exclaimed, "You both look so handsome."

Even though she looked at Nate, I'm sure she was talking about me. Just kidding. Nate did look handsome. He walked to the front desk to pick up the wicker basket with the satin pillow ready for the wedding rings. Usually plain, today it was decorated with silk flowers around the handle. Not fresh ones. Thank goodness. No sneezing.

The maid of honor came inside from the front porch and handed Nate the wedding rings. He placed the matching gold and diamond bands in the slits in the basket's satin pillow.

She smiled. "What a wonderful celebration and a happy day."

My ears shot up when I heard the pianist play. I pulled Nate to the large front windows to watch the guests all dressed up take their seats near the bottom of the staircase facing the wedding trellis. I recognized a few of them. Mr. and Mrs. Guyer held hands as they walked to their seats. And who's that under that gorgeous hat? Why it's Betty Brownet with Saul by her side in a suit and tie that coordinated with her outfit.

Meanwhile, I saw our staff still busy adjusting the silk flowers on the trellis to make sure everything was perfect. Nate and I walked outside to wait at the top of the front staircase for the rest of the bridal party. Four beautiful women in long satin gowns that matched my bowtie stood in front of me waiting to make their entrance. After a few minutes, the music changed to something I have heard before at weddings. Nate said, "That's our cue, 'The Wedding March'."

The guests stood and turned to watch the four women descend the staircase four stairs apart. Surprised, I saw Kate dressed in a matching gown at the bottom of the stairs wheel herself out to meet them. Her long curls jiggled and the smile on her face was beautiful. Jeff sat at the end of one aisle. By the look in his eyes, he was delighted to see Kate all dolled up make her entrance with the bridal party. He couldn't take his eyes off her as she wheeled herself down the aisle.

Then I heard the soft rustling of material behind me. That had to be the bride. When I turned to see who it was, I couldn't believe my eyes. It was Stephanie, looking more radiant and beautiful than I have ever seen her. She wore a long gown with lace sleeves and a long lace trimmed train.

When she came close to me, she leaned over and whispered, "Max, you're the reason for our joy today. I want to show you my something blue." Pinned to the inside of her bodice was my last year's metal dog license. Stephanie continued, "I'll always keep this tag close to my heart to remind me how much you changed my life and how much I love you."

I wanted to jump for joy, but Nate gave me "that look" which meant don't even think about it. I turned to see who was standing by the trellis. Yes! Yes! It was Aaron. I started to wag my tail so fast, happy to see Aaron, Nate had to quiet me down.

I understood. He placed the basket in my mouth, and we walked down the stairs together. Aaron gave me a wink before tears formed in his eyes as he watched my lovely Stephanie walk down the stairs and to the trellis. The ceremony was beautiful. The bride and groom beamed as they recited their vows.

Champagne fountains, a band, and loads of guests with

kids who couldn't wait to pet me made their reception the most amazing party I ever attended. I was in heaven. Aaron and Stephanie called me over to take a formal portrait with them. Stephanie had a small satin bag for me. What's this? I could smell doggie cannoli! Nate took the bag before I could get into it and thanked Stephanie as she and Aaron left for their first dance.

I turned toward the tent's entrance when I heard a woman's voice call out, "Hello? Wendy? Wendy where are you? The staff on the lawn said you were in here. I'd like to check in."

Of course, I had to pull away from Nate and run over to greet our newest guest. She was tall, thin, had light hair and was very tan. Older than Wendy, her left hand was tan enough to notice a ring missing. I sensed by her sad stare at the happy festivities she was in a world of hurt, so I sat up waiting for her to touch me. She looked down at me and smiled. I have the ability to do that for humans.

Wendy was not far behind me. "Mrs. Greene. Welcome. I was so sorry to hear about your husband's accident ten months ago. Please accept my deepest sympathy. I'll make sure you have the privacy and solitude you requested to grieve in peace. I see you've met Max, our canine concierge. I'll have to stay with him until Nate comes back to get him. We can then leave and go upstairs to the lobby to check you in."

Mrs. Greene nodded. "That's fine. Please call me Cheryl."

From where I stood, I saw Stephanie head to the band stand just as the band leader announced the tossing of the bridal bouquet. Stephanie stood at the very front of the stage with her back to the crowd of single women eager to catch her bouquet. She tossed the flowers from behind so high in the air they almost touched the tent's roof. I broke loose from Wendy and Cheryl to run in front of all those happy women and leap as high as I could to catch the bouquet in my teeth before it landed in any of their hands. I had a very special mission for those flowers.

The other guests laughed and applauded as I trotted with the flowers in my teeth to Kate, who watched from her wheelchair. I dropped the bouquet onto her lap. Everyone cheered my efforts. Kate was so surprised, she had to put her hands up to her face to cover some giggles. Excited, Jeff ran over to give her a big kiss.

Nate raced to Kate's chair to grab my leash to take me back to Wendy so she could leave to check in Cheryl. "Max, you are wonderful," Nate said. "You made Kate and Jeff so happy when you gave her the bouquet. I can't wait to see what you'll do next!"

Nate and I returned to Wendy just as I heard Cheryl tell her, "I wish them well. I lost the love of my life not too long ago, the best husband any woman could have, so I don't need or want another man in my life."

I tilted my head. Sure, Cheryl, we'll see about that, especially since I've heard that so many times before!

To answer Nate's question, I can't wait to see what I do next, either. I remain passionate about helping people feel better about themselves so they can open their hearts to love again. I adore Nate and someday hope to help him do just that. I love my job at Two Turtles Inn and want to stay here for a very long time.

THE END